SHARED PLEASURE

"You will see," he said. "One day you will know how truly I see the beauty in you."

He held her close in his arms, then gently pushed her back onto the grass. He braced himself over her, his weight on his elbows, and stared down at her, his long black hair brushing her breasts and tickling them. He lay along the length of her and she knew something momentous was about to happen.

She pulled him closer, eager to experience what awaited her. "Please," she begged, "make me a woman."

He threw back his head and laughed. "You are already a woman, Denai," he said. "A full woman. What I do is but share the pleasure with you."

She laughed too. "Come here, then," she crooned, "and show me that pleasure."

Theresa Scott

Love's Ambush

LEISURE BOOKS **NEW YORK CITY**

This book is dedicated to
Aisha Harrison and Michele Yoho,
daughters of my heart.

A LEISURE BOOK®

March 1997

Published by

Dorchester Publishing Co., Inc.
276 Fifth Avenue
New York, NY 10001

Copyright © 1997 by Theresa Scott

Printed in the United States of America.

With special thanks for technical consulting to:

Andy Appleby, Fisheries biologist, Olympia, WA;
Dr. John Fagan, Archeologist, Portland, OR;
Christopher Johnson, PA/SA, medical, Olympia, WA;
Dan Meatte, Archeologist, Olympia, WA.

Author's Note

This story is set 11,500 years ago near a group of archeology sites in what is now the middle of Oregon. Found at one of the sites were seventy-five pairs of sagebrush bark sandals thought to be between 7,000 and 13,200 years old. My characters wear similar sandals.

In North America at that time there lived woolly rhinoceros, camels, horses, giant sloths, giant bison, saber-toothed tigers, mammoths, mastodons, American lions, dire wolves and many other now-extinct life-forms.

The short-faced bear *(Arctodus)* was considered to be one of the largest and most powerful predators of that time. I have included this bear in the story and taken the liberty of giving it a very aggressive disposition. The short-faced bear is now extinct.

Love's Ambush

Prologue

Summer, 11,500 Years Ago
The North Edge of the Great Basin Area of North America

Blade strode along the gravel banks of a deep, slow-moving river. His sagebrush bark sandals slipped now and then on the wet, flat rocks. He gripped his spear tightly, his brown knuckles whitening. His strong jaw clenched and he brushed his long black hair out of his dark eyes.

Now that his temper had cooled somewhat, he had decided to return to the camp he shared with his faithless wife, Amethyst.

Earlier this day they had argued. Blade had demanded to know what Hunter, his former friend, had said to her yesterday when Blade had seen the two of them picking berries, their glossy black heads close

13

together, their hands touching as they placed handfuls of ripe berries in a basket. Even now the memory of them together made Blade's stomach knot in a jealous lump.

Amethyst had shrugged off Blade's demand; then, when he insisted he must know, she had whirled on him, screaming, "I made love with Hunter!" Her eyes blazing, she had snarled, "I would rather have your anger than your pity!"

Her words had hit him like a spear to his heart.

A black rage had come upon Blade then, and he had fled, fearing if he did not do so, he would surely hurt her, so angry was he. He had left her alone at their camp, the fire still burning, the brush hut only half-built.

He had run far away, as far away from her as he could get. Away from her and the knowledge that she wanted Hunter. Like a wounded lion, Blade had needed to find somewhere—anywhere—he might retreat. He needed to get away from her. Away from the pain of his searing jealousy. Away from the terrible wound to his heart.

Away from her.

And so he had left her alone at their camp. . . .

Now he was returning. He squinted at the sun. It had journeyed only a short distance on its midday path since he had been gone.

Blade's jaw clenched again, so tightly he could feel his jaw muscles throb. He closed his eyes, remembering her words anew. She had betrayed him.

Blade had loved her. Loved her!

He marched into camp. The hut was still half-finished. She had laid no more branches on the willow frame. The fire smoldered. Where was she?

"Amethyst!"

14

No answer.

"Amethyst!"

When she did not answer, he called out, "Come out, wife!"

But Amethyst did not appear.

He glanced around. The fire she had made was now embers; rabbit meat roasted on the coals. He sniffed. The rabbit meat was scorched. He went over and used a stick to push the carcass to a flat rock, where it would no longer burn. "Amethyst?" It was not like her to be so careless with meat. But he'd been mistaken before; he had thought she was a faithful wife to him, too. Now he knew better.

"Amethyst! Where are you?" He cast around, looking for her footprints. He saw prints leading to and from the river. Judging from the mixed, muddied prints, she had walked the short path between the camp and the river several times. He saw the filled water bladders near the fire. He touched them. They were warm to the touch. So the bladders had lain in the sun for some time then. She had been gone awhile.

"Amethyst!" He had thought his rage at her had cooled. But, not finding her, he felt himself grow angry again. Now was not the time to play foolish games hiding from him. Where was she?

"Amethyst?" He looked around, peering into their hut, walking through the tall grass near the river. Had she taken a nap somewhere? It was possible, but unlikely she would have slept so soon after their furious quarrel.

"Amethyst? Woman? Where do you hide?"

No answer. He searched the camp thoroughly now, taking in every footprint, every broken stem of grass. There were no footprints leading away from camp. It was as if a huge bird had swooped out of the sky and seized her, taking her away; so detailed was his search, so unexplainable her absence.

He pondered. When he had left, she, too, had been upset. He thought back on her words. *I made love to Hunter,* she had shrieked. *I would rather have your anger than your pity!* Why should Blade pity her for her betrayal with Hunter? That did not make sense. And she wanted his anger, did she? Well, she had seen it. Seen his shock, heard his rage-filled words as he shouted out his hurt, his anger at her betrayal.

She had turned from him then, his once beloved, once precious wife. She had presented her slim back and long black hair to him, as if in dismissal. That was when he knew he must leave her. Only for a time, until his rage cooled, but he must leave her, even though it meant leaving her alone when there were wolves and lions to watch out for. He had fled their camp.

"Amethyst?" Blade was quieter now, expecting no response.

She was gone. His wife of a few short moons was gone.

"She has returned to her parents' fireside," he muttered to himself. But a glance at their brush hut told him she had left her sewing things inside. If she was returning to the main Lion camp, would she not take her needles and awls and baskets?

"No!" His scream flew up to the sky and vanished. For a tiny moment the word *dead* had entered his brain. He did not want to think of such. A lion, or a saber-toothed tiger or a pack of wolves—had they seized her? But he had seen no such tracks and he had examined the ground minutely. She was gone. But not dead, surely not dead!

He walked over to the river and stared down into the clear green depths. The same river ran past the main Lion camp, too. He must return to his Lion People, he decided. He must see if Amethyst was there. Surely she was. She had to be.

He picked up his spear and her baskets and their few possessions. He kicked dirt over the smoking coals and the meat—he did not feel like eating anything right now. Her betrayal had sapped his appetite, leaving only a cold, hard knot in his gut.

He hurried along, following the river. He ducked aspen and willow branches and waded through freezing water. Now and then he stopped to call her name. His voice grew hoarse before he reached the Lion camp.

If she is back at her parents' fireside, he wondered, *should I convince her to return to me? What kind of a marriage will we have now that she has been unfaithful to me? I do not like this. I hate Hunter now. I think I hate Amethyst, too. How can I still want her for my wife?*

His gut pained him and his tight grip on his spear made his hand ache. His feet churned the black mud along the riverbank.

Ah, he would decide later. When he saw her. But of one thing he was certain. If they were going to resume their marriage, she must be faithful to him. No more Hunter.

Blade entered the Lion encampment at about the time of the evening meal. Pink and yellow streaks painted the western sky; the nights were short in the summer.

He reached his father's fireside and frowned

through the smoky blue haze. Where was everyone?
Where was Liontooth, his father?

Blade glanced around. At last he spied the Lion People—consisting of sixteen adults and nine children—clustered in a tense, excited group down by the river.

He walked toward them, scanning their sun-darkened faces for Amethyst's. He saw her father, Ochre, her mother, Obsidian, and even the old blind woman who constantly followed Obsidian about, but he did not see Amethyst.

As he approached, the muttering crowd parted to let a man walk through.

Blade straightened. Hunter marched toward him. Hunter, who had once been Blade's best friend—until they'd become rivals for Amethyst.

Blade stared. His heart pounded. In his arms Hunter carried a woman. Her head was flung back, revealing her long, pale throat. Her wet, black hair swept the ground with each step he took. She lay so limply in Hunter's arms, almost as though . . . she was . . . dead.

"Amethyst?" Blade blurted. He took a step toward Hunter. "Is it Am—" His words rammed against his throat and stopped.

"She is dead. Drowned." Hunter's brusque words cut like knives.

Blade gazed at his wife, and his fists clenched at his sides. She was dead! How could this be? What . . . ? How . . . ? It could not be! It could not! His mind reeled. His life was over. He stared at her, all thoughts of their argument gone. Amethyst. His beloved woman was dead!

How could he go on without her? There was no meaning in his life now. Nothing and no one would ever fill the horrible, gaping wound that her death had dealt him.

I should never have left her. The thought throbbed in his brain. *No matter how jealous I was . . .*

He stared dully at her lifeless body, wanting to take her in his arms just one last time, tell her he loved her and had not meant to say those cruel words. He had not meant to flee and leave her alone.

She could have Hunter. He would let her marry Hunter. He would not object. No, Blade would not stand in her way. If only she lived, if only she came back. *Oh, Amethyst . . .*

He closed his eyes and shook his head, not wanting to believe it was truly she. It could not be.

He opened his eyes and saw her limp body, saw Hunter's hate-filled dark eyes. She was dead. Truly dead. How had she been ripped away from him so suddenly? How?

He lifted his hand, intent suddenly on telling her, telling them all that he had wanted only to love her. . . .

But she was dead.

His hand dropped. Tears blurred his eyes and he brushed them away. At last his vision cleared enough for him to notice the crowd of Lion People staring at him.

He blinked back more tears. Everything that was precious in his life was gone.

Amethyst.

In Hunter's arms.

Blade clenched his fists. Bitter jealousy washed over his grief. Even in death it was Hunter who had her.

"Where were you?" Hunter demanded of Blade. His

voice was cold with loathing. Rage narrowed his black eyes.

Deep inside himself Blade felt his own rage stir. It was Hunter's fault, Blade told himself. It was Hunter who had caused that last furious argument between Blade and Amethyst. Hunter who had betrayed Blade's trust. Hunter whom Amethyst had loved.

And now she was dead.

Too late, he thought savagely. *I was too late. I should have returned sooner.*

"Where were you?" Hunter repeated.

Blade's eyes narrowed on Hunter, the man Amethyst had betrayed him for. But now, Blade thought hopelessly, neither one of us will ever have her.

"When I got back to our camp she was gone," Blade explained, his voice still hoarse from calling her name.

"You left her alone?" Ochre demanded in his deep voice. He and Obsidian, Amethyst's mother, crowded up behind Hunter.

Blade's fists clenched tighter. He did not need to be told he should never have left Amethyst alone. He knew it. There were lions and wolves and saber-toothed tigers. Fierce animals that could attack a lone woman.

Liontooth, Blade's father, shuffled over.

Blade's heart wrenched anew at the sight of his father. The old man's steps slowed more with each passing day. His back stooped closer to the ground with each passing moon.

Ochre and Obsidian glared at Blade. Four old women, one of them blind, scurried over to flank either side of Hunter. They hovered protectively over Amethyst's lifeless body. Clucking softly, they eased her body from Hunter's arms and carried her over to a brush hut. It was their task to prepare her for burial. The blind one stumbled as she carried one of Amethyst's legs. The others scolded her; she groped for the leg, lifted it and staggered off with the others.

"My son," Liontooth spoke up. His voice, unlike his body, was still strong. "We have found your wife. She was in the river—" Sorrow choked off his words.

Ochre pushed past Hunter and Liontooth and planted himself in front of Blade. Amethyst's father, Blade saw, shook with fury. His black eyes flashed. "My daughter is dead!" he cried. "You say you left her alone! Where were you? Why did you not help her? How is it that your clothes are dry? How is it that she came to be in the river, dead, and you are still alive? You did not even go into the water to save her!"

Blade could only stare at him. His throat worked, but no words came.

"No!" cried Obsidian. "Say nothing. There is nothing you can say. Words are too late. They cannot bring her back. Our daughter is dead!"

Blade's jaw clenched. How could he ever tell them what had happened?

"Look at him. He is here," Ochre said with a snarl, shaking his gray head from side to side in agony. "Liontooth's son is here. Alive. While our beloved daughter is dead!"

Blade wanted to scream out that he had loved Amethyst, that his loss was as great as—greater than— theirs. That Amethyst was his woman and no matter what had happened, he would always love her.

But the anguished words could not get past the lump of anger and guilt stuck in his throat.

Ochre whirled to face the gathered Lion People. He flung out his arms, gesturing wildly. "Do you want this

21

man to lead you?" he cried. "If you are lost or hurt, he will not come to your aid. He will abandon you as he did my daughter!"

Aghast, Blade saw several men nod their agreement at Ochre's words.

"Liontooth's son is not worthy!" Ochre continued. "He is not worthy to lead us! A man who cannot save his own woman has no claim upon the leadership of the brave Lion People!"

The onlookers murmured low amongst themselves. It was common knowledge that the Lion leaders always came from Blade's family. It had always been thus. Everyone knew that Blade would become headman after his father died. Blade had expected it ever since boyhood.

The bright black eyes of the Lion People shifted from Ochre to Blade and back again. Blade sensed their anger mounting against him. He must tell them what had happened. . . .

Liontooth stepped forward, stumbling in his haste. Blade caught him before he fell.

But after Liontooth pulled himself upright, he quickly thrust Blade's arm aside as if in no need of help. "The father of Amethyst is distraught," Liontooth said urgently. "He speaks without thinking."

Ochre swung to face the old man. "I do not! I speak the truth!"

The crowd stared at the two men: distraught Ochre and wary, frail Liontooth. A throbbing silence pulsed between them. Two men, two of the most skilled hunters of the Lion People, moved closer to Ochre.

Blade watched in dismay. The Lion men were turning against him—and worse, against his father. Blade realized they were angry and blamed him for Amethyst's death—he blamed himself more surely than they ever could—but now, to question his position as the next headman!

His gaze slid to his father. Liontooth had always been so proud of Blade, his only child. Early in Blade's life, his father had undertaken to teach Blade the skills needed to be headman.

Liontooth had spent much time with Blade. He'd taught him to listen carefully to quarreling people before giving his advice, to watch the seasons and the time when the geese flew to their homes in the south before deciding which caves the Lion People should winter in, to judge when the thickness of a rabbit's coat foretold a difficult winter ahead, and many other things a headman should know. And now? Liontooth looked pale and worried by Ochre's words.

"My son is a good man," proclaimed Liontooth. His voice sounded stronger. "Let my son speak. He has a right to defend himself."

Ochre glared at Blade as he sullenly waited for Blade to speak.

"It is true that I left Amethyst alone," began Blade sadly. "I left her at our camp. There was food—"

"He left my daughter to die!" cried Ochre.

Obsidian, Amethyst's mother, stumbled forward. She was sometimes called the Outsider because she had married into the Lion People long ago, so long ago no one remembered the name of her people, but they still occasionally called her the Outsider. She was a stout, mild-mannered woman who, as Blade's mother by marriage, had always treated him with respect and fixed deer stew the way he liked it.

Blade could see the fury in Obsidian's dark eyes. She spat full in his face.

Blade jerked back in surprise. With a shaking hand he wiped the spittle off his cheek.

"When he married my daughter," cried Obsidian, "he swore to protect her! To defend her with his life! Ha! How is it that she is dead? And he is alive? He must have run like a jackrabbit!"

Obsidian's words jabbed Blade like a spear. She had always been kind to him.

"I searched for her," he answered. "I looked for her footprints."

"Footprints, ha! He must leave our people!" cried Ochre in fury. "He is not fit to lead us!"

"Now, now, please," cried Liontooth in a shaking voice. "There will be no talk of my son leaving. Never has anyone—man or woman—been forced to leave the Lion People. He would die out in the hills alone. No, I say! He will stay!"

"He does not deserve to stay," Ochre said, snarling. Behind him several men shook their spears at Blade. "He left my daughter alone. By his own admission he left her alone! There are wolves out there. Huge bears. No man would leave his woman unprotected. He showed poor judgment!"

"Poor judgment, perhaps," admitted Liontooth cautiously. "But do not send a man away because of poor judgment. A man alone could never survive in the hills. You know that. I know that." He gestured at the listening people and raised his voice. "Not one of us would survive alone. Never, ever, have the Lion People abandoned one of their own!"

"He abandoned my daughter!" roared Ochre, his words dropping one by one like huge stones into the still waters of a lake. "He would abandon the Lion People in the same way!"

Alarmed, Blade glanced around. Threatening black gazes met his eyes. His heart sank. They did not want him. Worse, he could understand their fear.

"True, your daughter is dead, Ochre," said Liontooth, edging closer to Blade. Even Blade could hear the trembling in his father's deep voice. "We are all most sorrowful about her death. But this does not mean my son must step aside as the next leader. Why, the leadership of the Lion People belonged to my father and his father before him. My family's sons have always been the leaders of the Lion People. Do you not remember?" Blade cringed inwardly at the begging note in his father's voice.

Ochre glowered fiercely and shook his spear at Liontooth. "Then it is time to change," he said with menace.

"You know I am getting old," Liontooth pleaded. "The Lion People need a man who is young, a man who is strong to lead them. My son is—"

"Let Hunter or one of the other young men lead," interrupted Ochre rudely. "Let a man lead who deserves the honor. A man who is strong, and defends his loved ones. A man who will not run and save only himself!" Ochre spat on the ground. "I do not care if he is your son. My daughter is dead!" He glared at Liontooth. "Your son must leave!"

Loud murmurs from the other Lion men greeted Ochre's demand.

"He would make a poor leader," said one with a snarl.

"He should have saved his woman," Hunter said in a ringing voice.

Blade whirled on him. "You have much to gain from this, you who would be headman if I left."

25

Hunter sneered. "I would make a better headman than you, *friend*. I would never leave a defenseless woman."

Guilt rocked Blade. He took a step back. The realization hit him like a hard blow to his stomach. She was dead. *What have I done? Oh, Amethyst! What in the Great Mother's name have I done?*

"The father of the dead woman"—Blade could not bring himself to speak Amethyst's name for fear he would weep and shame himself further in front of the Lion People—"is correct," he croaked. "I am not worthy to lead the Lion People."

"My son," implored Liontooth, "do not say this. A terrible thing has happened. But you can still lead."

Blade turned away. He could hear the trembling hope in his father's voice, hope he must kill. He had no right to his father's hope.

"Where are you going, my son?" Liontooth asked, reaching out a hand to stop him.

"I must leave."

"No!" cried Liontooth. "Ochre means you would not be headman, not that you must leave our people!" A father's anguish was in the headman's cry.

"He should leave!" Ochre said angrily. "Why should we have to face his daily presence? His constant reminder that he ran, and left my daughter to die?"

"Cruel words," answered Liontooth heatedly. His wrinkled face flooded red as he rallied to fight for his only son.

"Cruel, perhaps, but true," Ochre assured him bitterly. "Does your son dispute my words?" He glared at Blade and Blade could see the rage in the old man's eyes. "Speak up. Dispute my words if you can. But I

26

know I speak the truth. I know you did not protect my daughter."

"My son did not run," Liontooth protested.

"I do not dispute your words," Blade affirmed quietly.

A hushed stillness fell upon the gathered people as they gazed at Blade. Hunter's black, loathing look stood out among them all.

Blade could face their condemnation no longer. He turned his back and walked away from them.

"My son!" cried Liontooth. "Stop! You cannot go."

"I must, Father. They do not want me to lead them. They do not even want me to live with them."

His father hurried to catch up to him. "My son, do not go. This will pass. You can stay. You will be headman. I will help you. My father before me . . ."

Blade met his father's hopeful eyes. His fingers curled around Liontooth's arms. "Father, you must listen to me. They do not want me," he said deliberately.

"But, my son, where will you go? Who will you go with? Who will be your companions?"

"No one," Blade said grimly. "My memories of Amethyst will be my companions."

His father dropped his earnest gaze and his shoulders slumped. Defeat settled heavily on the old man's tired features. "Then if you must go, take some smoked meat with you, my son. You will find it in my hut."

Blade nodded at the dull acceptance he heard in his father's voice. He veered toward Liontooth's brush shelter.

It is true, Blade thought as he gathered up several pieces of smoked meat. *I did run. Not in the way they think, but I ran. I was gone when Amethyst needed me!*

27

He had his few possessions: his spear, a hunting bag that held his tool kit of rocks, and his sacred power bag. He left Amethyst's sewing basket in his father's hut. Liontooth would know to give it to Obsidian and Ochre later.

He went to bid his father farewell. All talking ceased when Blade strode up to Liontooth. The hostile Lion men watched him, spears gripped tightly.

I could never lead these Lion People now, Blade thought. *They do not trust me. And without the trust of his people, a leader is useless; my father taught me that. What could I tell them? They can see that I am alive, and Amethyst is dead. That is all that matters to them.*

Liontooth came to meet him. "Do not go, my son. You go to certain death." His father's dark eyes implored Blade in a way his words could not. "No one can survive alone out in the hills, the vast lands. You need people."

Blade held up a hand to ward off his father's powerful plea. "Hush. I must go, Father."

Liontooth's brown eyes met Blade's sorrowfully.

"I cannot stay, Father," Blade said in a low voice. "You know that. It is better to take my chances alone than to live with our people. They would grow to distrust me, fear me and hate me." He glanced around. "They do now."

His father peered at the glowering Lion People. "It is true," he acknowledged sadly. "Go then," he whispered at last. "I will not stop you." He stepped aside, out of Blade's path. Head bowed, he stumbled toward his brush shelter.

Blade turned to go.

"See!" Ochre cried. "Liontooth's son leaves! He will not even stay to see her buried! That's what kind of husband he is. Abandon her in life. Abandon her in death!" Ochre's scorn ripped like a sharp knife across Blade's raw heart-wound.

With a grimace, Blade faced his dead wife's father. Ochre's trembling mouth and narrowed eyes told the story of his grief and anguish—the same pain that throbbed in Blade's heart. Amethyst's death was a terrible loss to her father and mother, too. The angry words Blade meant to speak died in his throat.

And he realized he had no words that would heal his father by marriage's anger and grief. To say anything would only hurt Ochre more. Blade turned away.

Ochre spat at Blade in disgust. So did several of the other men. Blade flinched in humiliation. Spittle landed on his bare chest, his arms, his leather breechcloth, his legs.

"My son," Liontooth said, hurrying from his brush home. He halted when he saw the men spitting on his son. He approached slowly, head high, as though he saw naught of what they did. "My son," he said, drawing Blade away from the men, "I must give you something.

"Open your hand." Ignoring the gawking men, Liontooth placed a large piece of black stone in Blade's palm. "Take this piece of obsidian with you. It belonged to my father, and his father before him. It came from a faraway quarry, a most excellent quarry. Neither your grandfather nor your great-grandfather were ever able to find that place again. But look! The quality of this obsidian rock surpasses the best I have ever seen. It makes excellent weapons." He pressed Blade's fist around the chunk of shiny black rock. "Take it and use it, my son. It will always protect you."

The rock was cold and hard and smooth in Blade's hand. He nodded his thanks silently to his father. The two men embraced.

Blade touched the small, sacred power bag that hung at his chest. Inside were the sacred feathers, sacred rocks and precious things that had accompanied him since his first vision quest.

Carefully, he removed the sacred power bag from around his neck. "I give this to you, my father. The Great Mother no longer protects me or mine. I am cut off from Her now. I wander alone."

"My son, do not say such things," Liontooth cried in alarm, trying to push the power bag back into Blade's hand. "To say such things invites the Great Mother's wrath!"

Blade shook his head slowly. "I have already felt the Great Mother's wrath—Amethyst is lost to me; my people are lost to me." His lips tightened as he choked back words. "I will say no more than this: I want no more of the Great Mother or her power. I speak the truth on this."

Liontooth bowed his head, but not before Blade saw the tears in his eyes.

Head held high, Blade surveyed the Lion People for a long moment. Even now, forced to leave them, he wanted to remember their names and faces. Perhaps, with time, their memory would be a consolation to him, during the time alone that would mark the remainder of his life.

He caught Hunter's furious glower. There would be no consoling memory of Hunter, thought Blade angrily.

Lastly, Blade turned to look upon his father's craggy, wrinkled face. He banished angry thoughts from his mind at this, his final time with his father. Liontooth was old. No doubt this was the last time Blade would look upon his father's countenance.

He squeezed the cold, smooth rock in his hand. It was from his great-grandfather—his father's father's father. At least he had this rock to take with him.

Blade took a step away from Liontooth. And then another one. Then another step. He had lived with the Lion People since his birth twenty-two summers before. Once he had thought he'd been destined to lead them. But no more. Not now. Not after Amethyst's death.

Henceforth Blade would walk alone, leading no one and carrying his shame with him out into the hills.

He took another reluctant step. Even now a part of him wanted to hear the Lion People call him back. Someone. Anyone. If even one of the Lion People called him back, he would return. He knew it, felt the fear of leaving them knotting in his stomach. There was nothing out in the hills for him. Only loneliness and death.

But no one called his name. He kept walking.

I never got to tell her good-bye.

Chapter One

Summer, Two Years Later

"Where is your brother?" asked Rabbit Woman in a falsely sweet voice. She and Pika glared at Denai. Rabbit Woman tossed her long black hair and smoothed her knee-length woven sagebark skirt. Pika picked a loose thread off Rabbit Woman's rabbitskin top.

Denai sat cross-legged on the ground and scraped at the deer hide on the wooden frame in front of her. She was not fooled by Rabbit Woman's falsely kind manner.

"Which brother?" Denai asked, her hands moving wearily across the hide, scraping, scraping. "I have three."

Rabbit Woman's thin lips tightened. "Trout. Your youngest brother." Her voice was not so sweet this time.

Rabbit Woman had long wanted Trout for a husband, and Denai knew she would stop at nothing to get him.

"He is gone," Denai answered slowly. She brushed her heavy black hair off her forehead. It was so warm today! She yawned, feeling so tired. And nothing interested her anymore, not even Rabbit Woman's relentless pursuit of Trout.

"When will he be back?" Rabbit Woman's voice dripped with impatience. Denai frowned. She should be used to the resentment in the other Willow maiden's manner by now. For some reason, Rabbit Woman expected that Denai should help her in her chasing after Trout. After all, there were only a few eligible males in the Willow camp, and Rabbit Woman considered Trout to be the best. Pika, Rabbit Woman's constant companion, wanted Dirk, Denai's second brother. Flint, Denai's oldest brother, apparently held no interest for either Willow maiden.

As one of the three unmarried females in the Willow camp, Rabbit Woman considered herself the most desirable. And with her long black hair, her plump frame, and her flashing black eyes, she was correct to do so, thought Denai.

Pika was also lovely to look upon, unlike herself, thought Denai with only a pinch of regret.

Denai went about with her long hair tied back, or knotted carelessly. She wore a dull brown rabbitskin top that had already seen three seasons. Her woven sagebark skirt was too short and her sandals too thick and clumsy. But Denai did not care how she appeared. There were no men in this Willow camp she wanted to marry. None. Not after Chert died.

Denai summoned an inward shrug as she continued

to scrape the deer hide. Out of the corner of her eye she saw Rabbit Woman stamp her bare feet, irritated. And Pika made a silent face at Denai.

Denai pretended not to notice. It appeared that Rabbit Woman would soon burst with her impatience, so Denai answered, "Trout will return this eve."

"Humph." Rabbit Woman snorted. "If he was not your brother, I would not spend one moment speaking with you."

Denai looked up from her scraping. "I know that," she answered calmly.

"No one would speak with you," Pika assured Denai. Her high-pitched voice sounded like a little girl's, but her manner was that of a petulant young woman. "Except to tell you to take care of the children. Or fetch the water. That is all you are good for." She giggled.

With a sly smile, Rabbit Woman drew back her foot and kicked Denai on the shin. Denai winced. Pika laughed.

"Do not think to tell anyone I did that," said Rabbit Woman, her sweet voice returning. "Especially not Trout. If you do, I will tell him you lie."

Her eyes glittered like shards of obsidian. "Your brothers must get very tired of hunting and bringing meat to you," Rabbit Woman continued, seething. "You, who are a grown woman, you are old enough to marry a man of your own who will hunt for you! You are naught but a burden on your brothers, do you know that?" Rabbit Woman leaned closer and angry spittle glistened on her lower lip. "Find a man to marry so that your brothers are free to take wives!"

Pika snorted. "Hunh. No man wants her." She picked up a small handful of dirt and cast it on the deer hide that Denai had been scraping. Dust blew in Denai's eyes. When she could see again, she leaped to her feet, but Pika and Rabbit Woman were already laughing and running away.

Her pride smarting, Denai sat down again and continued her task, careful to remove all the small bits of grit on the hide. When would she learn to ignore the baiting words of Rabbit Woman and Pika? They were jealous that her brothers cared for her, that was all, Denai told herself. But if her brothers cared for her, then why did Rabbit Woman's words cut so deeply?

A twinge of fear entered Denai's heart. What if Rabbit Woman was correct? What if she was a burden to her brothers?

Her lips tightened and she pushed the foolish thoughts away. Her brothers loved her! They wanted to hunt for her. She was not a burden. She was not!

Before the accident with the short-faced bear, Rabbit Woman would never have dared to speak so to Denai. Not when Denai was the beloved betrothed of Chert, the best hunter in the Willow camp.

Denai's hands flew to cover her face. *Oh, Chert!* How she missed him—his kindness, his tenderness toward her. He would have made a gentle, loving husband—if the short-faced bear had not killed him first.

Hot tears poured down her cheeks. Chert, her betrothed—and the only eligible man who wanted to marry her. Since the accident and his death, not one Willow man had gone to her brothers with a request for her hand. Not one, she thought in sudden anguish. But why should they? And why should she care?

Denai wiped away the tears, using her soft black hair to do so. There were only two or three eligible Willow men to marry anyway. There was the shaman

35

and a young man named Squirrel, who hunted with her brothers occasionally. And Turtle was always saying he wanted a second wife. The trouble was, his first wife would pull his hair whenever he spoke of it. And none of the men made Denai's blood warm as Chert had. None.

Few of the Willow People even spoke to her anymore—because of the bear accident, she supposed. Chert had died protecting her. While he fought the bear, she had hidden in a small rock shelter, and the rampaging bear had passed her by.

It was after the accident that she began to notice the awkward silence that would fall upon a group of women or men whenever she approached. By now she had come to accept that sudden silence as punishment for Chert's death.

At least she had her brothers. They were loyal to her. Ever since their parents' deaths when she was a child of five summers, her brothers had protected Denai and cared for her. They had hunted meat for her, even taught her to hunt recently when it became painfully apparent to them, too, that no man was going to offer for her. They helped carry her possessions whenever camp was moved. They made sure she had enough hides for her winter shelter. *Eeyak*, yes, they were good brothers to her in every way. They had been very kind to her since the accident with the bear.

Aaiiee, the wretched bear, thought Denai sadly. Oh, how her life had changed after the vicious short-faced bear had killed Chert. She now saw the bear as a power in her life, an evil power, a power that had reached out and wreaked an arc of destruction on her whole life the day it felled Chert with one cruel blow of its claws.

Her people called the short-faced animal Evil One. He was well named, to Denai's mind. He was bad tempered and easily recognizable, a huge creature with a ragged patch of naked brown skin on his right flank. She still saw him in her nightmares.

She continued to scrape the deer skin methodically. At least she had her precious brothers—the youngest, playful Trout, then shy Dirk, then stern Flint, the eldest. These brothers would hunt and provide meat for her for the rest of their lives. All three of them.

Denai smiled to herself. If Rabbit Woman knew how highly her brothers regarded their only sister, she would pull out every one of Denai's long black hairs in vengeful retribution. But Rabbit Woman did not know.

Denai stopped scraping and inspected the hide. Perhaps she would make a fine pair of moccasins out of this hide. Dirk needed new moccasins. Trout needed a shirt. And Flint? Flint was due for a pair of leggings for the cold winters.

Denai thought for a moment. The deer hide she was scraping was small. It would be moccasins for Dirk, then.

As she scraped she wondered if she should mention Rabbit Woman's pursuit to Trout—again. *Dak,* no. No need to, she decided. Trout would never marry Rabbit Woman. If he wanted her he would have chosen her by now. And he had not.

Denai sighed pensively. She could not bring herself to pursue a man the way Rabbit Woman did. Instead she had resigned herself to the fact that no Willow man wanted her. That was fine with her. She would spend the rest of her life taking care of the Willow children. And weaving her baskets. And sewing.

She mused on how strange it was that she, in her full prime, should find herself so alone. Alone and unwanted.

Her pensive thoughts were interrupted as the shaman, Wild Dog, walked by. He glared at her but said nothing. She found herself cringing inside from that single look. Why was this fear of Wild Dog growing inside her breast? she wondered.

She flushed and continued her scraping. Wild Dog hated her. She knew that because he did not try to hide it. She had often wondered what she had done to him to deserve such hatred. He had wanted to marry her at the same time Chert had offered for her. Though Wild Dog had offered better gifts, it was Chert whom Denai had accepted. And then Chert had been killed.

And now there would be no marriage for Denai. Ever. And there would be no children, either.

Her hands fell idle for a moment. Ah, children. Her heart ached. That was her one regret. She would have found joy in having children.

Why had everything gone so wrong? she wondered, stroking her woven sagebark skirt sadly. No one spoke to her; there was no one to marry or who wanted to marry her, so there was no hope of ever having children.

At the thought of children, she picked up the scraper again and drew it back and forth over the deer hide, scraping the fat with almost feverish strokes.

It was enough that she looked after the children of her neighbors, she told herself insistently. Sometimes she walked the children to the river to swim, or out into the hills. Or played with them while their mothers went berry-picking. The children liked her. *Eeyak*, yes.

Tears stung her eyes. That was the only way that Denai would ever have children; she had come to realize it—to accept it—since the accident. She would look after the children of other women and it would suffice. It would have to.

She glanced up at the sun, her vision blurred by her futile tears. Soon her brothers would return from their hunting trip. They would be hungry. She must make them a fine stew—one befitting them and showing them that she was grateful.

Chapter Two

Blade landed with a thud on his injured shoulder. He groaned and tried to sit up, but his bound hands and feet made his movements awkward. One of his captors kicked him back down in the dirt. He fell heavily. His shoulder throbbed.

Frozen from the pain, Blade tried to get his bearings. Every part of his body ached from the fight he had been through. And all he could see now were bare feet and a forest of brown legs crowded around him. He glared through the tangle of his black hair at the curious fools staring down at him.

It had all happened so swiftly. Only this morning he had built his solitary brush shelter and then sat down to carefully chip tiny flakes off an obsidian spear point. Concentrating intently, he had not heard the three men creep up on him. The men who had ambushed him were ruggedly built, tough and, like him, wore only leather breechcloths.

Though Blade fought with all his might and strength, the three had finally overpowered him, gagged him, tied his wrists with leather bonds and marched him a full day's travel to this encampment.

Blade shook the mass of his long black hair out of his eyes so he could see better. He winced from the pain in his shoulder. He had wrenched it when he'd grabbed the stocky one, the shortest of his captors, and flung him head over heels to the ground. With a grimace, Blade remembered that it was after that throw that the fight had turned truly nasty.

The people around him began murmuring. He strained to hear. He found, despite their strange pronunciation, that he could recognize most of their words if he listened closely.

"Ho! Here comes Denai. Why does Flint bring her over here?"

"She does not want to come," observed a woman. "See, he pulls her along."

"She is a mouse, a dull mouse," added another woman. "She creeps around our camp. When she is not watching the children, she hides in her hut all day. Ever since—"

"Hush, Rabbit Woman," interrupted another feminine voice. "You know her brothers are very protective of her. Trout would not like to hear you speak against her."

"I only speak the truth," insisted Rabbit Woman in a sullen tone.

Blade glanced around. Two of his captors stood near him; the other was guiding a woman in Blade's direction.

I have to get out of here, he thought. But no oppor-

41

tunity to escape had yet presented itself under the watchful black eyes of his three strong captors.

Muscles aching, Blade drew his legs up. A plan formed quickly in his brain. While the crowd's attention was upon the man and woman coming toward them, he would escape. He got to his knees; no one heeded his movements, since they were all watching the woman. He pushed himself halfway up. Then a foot tripped him and he fell back down in the dust.

"You stay there." His thickly set young captor laughed. Blade glared at him. The man grinned, his brown eyes gleaming in amusement.

Blade shook his head. Ever since his capture he'd studied his three captors, determined to learn something about them that would aid his escape. All he'd learned thus far, he realized in disgust, was their names and that this particular captor, Trout, liked to joke and laugh.

The people clustered around Blade guffawed.

He gritted his teeth. He would escape these fools!

His tall, thin captor, named Dirk, stood watchfully silent, as always, his arms across his bare chest. Blade followed his glance.

"We went to much trouble to catch him," Flint explained to the woman. A thick-shouldered man, his long hair was turning gray at the temples of his wide, brown face. He appeared to be the eldest of Blade's three captors, and, as they bore a family resemblance to each other, Blade guessed them to be brothers.

"He put up a good fight," said Trout. He said it so proudly that Blade glanced at him. "He is very strong, Denai."

Blade eyed the woman. Her body was slim and she wore a woven sagebark skirt and short tunic of brown rabbitskin. Her dainty feet were shod in woven sage-bark sandals that tied crisscross on her shins. Her black hair was tied back in a loose horsetail style. Her face was turned away from him as she spoke to the eldest. "Who?" she asked softly. "Who is he? Why did you bring him here?"

"He is to be your husband," answered Flint.

The woman jerked her head and turned to face Blade, her jaw dropping. Then someone's legs blocked his view. "Husband?" The woman's astonishment was no match for Blade's.

Trout laughed delightedly. Dirk grinned slowly, his eyes on the woman.

Blade inhaled. Did they mean him? He was to be her husband? He peered up through the thicket of legs, striving to get a better view of her. Amused faces stared down at him. The people wore long black hair, woven sagebark clothes, light fur capes and vests. The married women wore colorful beaded net caps on their heads. Not so different from how his own people dressed in summer. But he did not know them. They were strangers.

His view of the woman was still blocked.

"I do not want a husband!" She sounded almost angry.

Relief rushed through him. He was glad to hear that she did not want him, for he did not want her. He wanted no woman ever again. Ever.

He lay as though carved from wood, while the crowd's attention fastened on the woman and Flint. He had wondered at the time of his capture why they did not simply kill him. Now he knew.

He noticed she was slightly built and her hair was

severely drawn back. How plain. Amethyst had been beautiful—and deceitful.

The woman still faced away from Blade. A large man in the crowd moved aside and at last Blade could see her.

There was anger in every line of her trembling body as she leaned toward Flint. *"Dak,* no! I do not need a husband."

"You need someone to hunt for you," Trout said.

She whirled on him. "I have you, my three brothers," she protested. "You get all the meat I need. I do not need . . . him." She reeled around once more and pointed at Blade.

He strained to look at her. He was only curious, he assured himself.

Her features contorted in bewilderment. She saw him looking at her and held his gaze. Her brown eyes flashed. Her delicate nose turned up at the sight of him and her chin quivered. Her full lips were set in a stubborn line. *"Dak,* I will not have him!" she burst out.

Blade gritted his teeth and eyed her slim form insolently. *Not have me?* His jaw tightened. *Be assured I feel as you do, woman!* But the leather gag in his mouth prevented his speech.

Her face turned red at his slow perusal. "Take him back," she added, her chin jutting out stubbornly.

"We cannot," spoke up Dirk. "We, uh, found him. He is ours. And we give him to you, Denai."

But Denai was resolute. "His people—they will want him back."

"He has no people," answered Dirk.

"That is correct," added the young, thickset Trout. "He was alone when we, uh, found him. No people."

They tell her only part of the truth, thought Blade.

They did not find me; they ambushed me! As for no people, that much is true. It has been two years and I have no plans to return to the Lion People. Ever.

Flint, the eldest brother, spoke again. "He will be your husband, Denai. We are tired of providing you with meat. Let him do so now."

There were giggles in the crowd from two young women. Denai whirled to stare at their simpering faces; then she faced her brother again.

"You would humiliate me in front of our people?" she cried as if stunned.

"Humiliate you, Denai?" said Trout. "We do not humiliate you." He glanced around at the avid faces and cleared his throat. "We do not do this to humiliate you, Denai," he said gently. "We do it to provide you with a husband. We are your brothers and as such it is our duty—"

"I do not want a husband!" came Denai's angry reply. She glared at Blade as though he had caused this predicament. He glared back.

"He is to be your husband," said Flint firmly.

"*Dak,*" she answered, pulling her gaze back to her brother. "I will not have him!" She stomped off.

Blade made a noise through the gag they had tied over his mouth. He wanted a chance to speak. He would tell these fools that, in spite of her spirit, he did not want her either.

Unwillingly, he watched the woman walk away. She turned around.

Though her body was lithe and graceful, it was her flashing eyes he watched. Yet, in spite of those eyes, it was a very plain face she had. Hers was not the lush, exciting beauty of Amethyst. Then he quickly shut out the thought of Amethyst.

Dak, there was nothing about this woman he wanted. *Will no man have her? Why must her brothers hunt down a man for her?* he wondered. *No matter their reason, it will not be me!*

Determined to get away from these people and the woman, he struggled anew against the tight leather bonds on his wrists. He grimaced from the pain. The leather did not loosen. He was well and truly bound.

"How could they do this?" muttered Denai as she raced back to her brush shelter. "How could they? My brothers! My own brothers! They are supposed to help me. Protect me . . ."

She wanted to run out into the hills and hide until her feelings of humiliation vanished. Although it was true that, since her parents had died, she had relied upon her brothers to supply her with meat, she had not thought their duty so onerous, so disgusting that they would refuse to do it any longer. Yet that was what they were telling her. *We are tired of providing you with meat. Let him do so now.* Flint's cruel words rang in her memory even now.

Why, she had thought they loved her, and wanted to provide for her! And now this!

Her lips tightened. Very well. She would provide her own meat from this time on. She knew how to hunt, knew how to throw a spear and kill a deer. She had learned to do so after the accident. Trout had taught her to hunt. Trout, her youngest brother, her joking brother—his betrayal hurt most of all.

These brothers of hers, men she thought she knew, men she had trusted all her life, these now worthless brothers had hunted down a stranger and thrown him at her, like—like a bison rib bone. What was the matter with them?

Once in the circle of safety of her brush hut, she sank to her knees and sobbed. How could her brothers do this to her? They had humiliated her in front of all the Willow People! *Eeyak*, yes, she had heard the giggles of Rabbit Woman and Pika. How they had laughed.

Denai cried bitter tears. They were only jealous, she told herself over and over. Jealous.

She touched her burning cheeks. Her fingers came away wet. She could not lie to herself. It was not jealousy, no matter how much she wished it so. *Dak*, it was not jealousy but happy delight. Once her brothers cast her off onto some man, they would be free to take wives—wives like Rabbit Woman and Pika.

She squeezed her eyes shut, trying to shut out the shame. Was she such a pitiful woman that her brothers must hunt down a husband for her?

Somewhere deep inside her, a small voice answered *eeyak*, yes. She writhed on the woven reed mats on the floor of the hut. *Dak*, it was not true! Her life was good. She had her weaving, her basketry work. She had her brothers to sew for. She took care of the children when their mothers went berry-picking or to the creek. Was that not enough for any woman?

Dak, no, answered the same horrid little voice.

"But it is enough for me!" she cried aloud.

Only the singing of crickets met her lying words.

"It must be enough for me." She sobbed. "It must!"

For who knew better than she what her life held? Who knew better than she the lifelessness within her own breast? Lifelessness that had arrived the day the great short-faced bear, Evil One, had killed Chert and with one cruel blow of his huge paw had stolen forever Denai's hopes and dreams. Chert, her beloved; Chert, the gentle. Chert was gone.

She touched her wet face. Who in this camp cared about her? Certainly not her brothers. They had proven that this day. If they cared about her, they would continue to hunt for her, not cast her off on this—this stranger.

And the stranger? What must he think? She had caught only a glimpse of him—his tangled hair, his bruised, dirt-encrusted, long-limbed body. She would not think about him, not at all. Her brothers must take him back to wherever it was they had found him. Then she would never have to worry about any wild stranger coming into her life—nor be tormented by these new and hopeless thoughts.

Thoughts of a husband, of children . . .

Chapter Three

"Denai! Come out!"

Inside the hut, Denai froze. What did Flint want? Had he sent the stranger away?

Denai wiped the tears from her face and sat up, careful not to rustle the woven reeds she lay upon. She did not want her brother to know she had been crying.

"Denai!"

"*Eeyak?* What is it you want?"

"Come out here." Flint's voice was firm.

She heard someone giggling outside the hut. *Rabbit Woman and Pika,* she thought irritably. *Happy to see me humiliated.*

The mere thought of giving those two women something more to laugh at compelled Denai to rise to her knees.

"Denai." It was Trout's voice now. "Come out. We want you to come out here."

49

More giggling.

Lips tight, Denai wondered if she should go out and see what was so amusing to Rabbit Woman, or if she should just hide in her brush hut and pretend her wretched brothers were not calling to her. Her suspicions were definitely aroused. If two of her brothers wanted her out there, and Rabbit Woman was amused, Denai knew it meant trouble. For her.

"Oh Denaaaaiiii," Rabbit Woman sang. "Your brothers want to speak with yooooouuuu."

Denai decided she must remember to tell Rabbit Woman how overly sweet her voice was, like honeydew, the crystallized dung droppings of aphids and whiteflies that the Willow women gathered from cattail reeds every summer.

She poked her head outside the hut. "Go away," she whispered. She paused. Staring at her was every man, woman and child of the Willow People, not just her two brothers and Rabbit Woman. Denai popped her head back in the hut, hid her face in her hands and moaned. Oh, what was she going to do?

"Denai." Flint sounded embarrassed now, and angry. Rabbit Woman's simpering giggles did not help matters. Denai shrugged. So Flint did not like her staying in the hut? Well, she did not like him demanding she leave the hut!

"Denai, if you do not come out I will come in and drag you out!"

Rabbit Woman laughed, and others joined in with guffaws.

Denai shut her eyes and groaned. Let them laugh. She would not come out. Whatever they wanted, it was not good—for her. "*Dak!* I will not come out."

"You will," Flint said. She could hear his footsteps

50

approach the hut. She huddled in a tight ball on the woven reeds, and kept her back to the door.

His strong hands gripped her on the arms and he pulled her. She stayed in a tight ball. "I did not hunt down that man so you could hide away," he said, panting, dragging her across the woven mats.

As they reached the threshold she flailed her arms about. "*Dak, dak!* I do not want to come out!" she cried.

"*Eeyak!* You will," Flint answered firmly. "You cannot hide in here all day."

Denai wanted to—oh, how she wanted to. But they were outside now and she remained crouched in a ball.

"Get up," he demanded.

She peeked at the feet surrounding her. Slowly she rose, keeping her eyes on the ground. She would not meet the staring eyes of her people, nor glance at Rabbit Woman's amused face.

"She is such a mouse," Rabbit Woman muttered, her pretty face pinched, almost ugly. The crowd stirred.

The decision-maker and headman of the Willow People, Denai's uncle Rhino, pushed his way through the knot of people. "Do not hide your face, child," he said kindly.

Denai wanted to weep at the kindness in her mother's brother's voice. But she did not. She continued to stare at the ground. "I want to go back in the hut," she whispered.

"Your brothers have found you a husband," her uncle said. "Come and see him."

She shook her head and dug her heels firmly into the dirt. "I have seen him, Uncle. I-I do not want him."

51

"Denai," Flint said, "listen to me, your eldest brother." He took a step away from her and raised his arms to address the gathered Willow People. "My brothers and I have hunted for you. Ever since our parents died when you were just a young girl, we have given you meat. We have watched over you, protected you from the wolves and lions."

He glanced at her. "We would have protected you and Chert from the bear if we could have," he said heavily.

Wild Dog, who was fire-keeper and shaman, stepped forward. "Chert tried to protect her from the bear," he said in a cold voice. "Chert died protecting her, and he was the strongest hunter of our Willow People. It is her fault he died!"

At the shaman's words, Denai shrank into herself. There was muttering among the Willow People about Chert's death. She heard someone say, "Chert's life was wasted on her." Humiliated, she backed toward the hut, intent on getting away from everyone.

She heard Flint bark, "Denai did not cause Chert's death! That is a lie the shaman tells you! His death was an accident!" There was grumbling at his words, but no one contradicted him.

Then Flint's hand shot out and gripped her arm while he continued steadily, "Denai, raising you has weighed heavily upon us, your brothers. Not one of us has taken a wife nor fathered children because we wanted you to grow strong. We wanted to care for you until you were grown."

He regarded her and she saw the satisfaction in his brown eyes—satisfaction, and something else. Sadness?

"You are a woman grown now." He touched his own

gray hair. "We are getting older. If we would take wives it must be now, so that we may enjoy our children while we are still strong and able to hunt."

Denai wanted to weep at how badly she had misjudged her brothers' efforts. She had thought they wanted to care for her. Now she was learning that they felt they had to care for her. And they did not want to do it any longer.

Eeyak, she could understand their needs now, too. Humiliation at her own selfishness in keeping them from mates and children swept over her, and she hid her face in her hands.

She tried to swallow. The thick lump in her throat did not move.

There was a rustling at the back of the crowd. A disturbance grew. "Bring him forth," ordered Flint. "Look, Denai."

Reluctantly she dropped her hands.

The crowd parted to let Dirk through. Trout hurried over to him. Between them, still gagged and with his hands bound, struggled the stranger.

My husband, she thought, and a shiver went through her. *They want to make this man my husband!*

She watched Dirk's slow movement through the crowd. Twice the stranger tried to pull away, but Dirk held on tightly to his arm. Once he tried to run, but Trout barred his way.

Both her brothers were panting by the time they reached the front of the crowd. The stranger's broad brown chest heaved and fell, too, but she quickly averted her eyes. Uncle Rhino stepped aside to let them pass.

"We cleaned him up for you, Denai," said Dirk proudly.

She focused only on Dirk and Trout. She would not look at the stranger. She would not!

"I . . . I . . ." Her voice was a mere whisper. Oh, how she wanted to be as firm and as confident as Flint was. To be as amused as Trout was. But her words faltered. "I—I do not want him."

"Look at him, Denai," Trout said encouragingly. Instead of staring at the stranger, however, she kept her gaze on Trout. Of all her brothers, his betrayal was the most bitter. She had thought she could depend on him, but he was as eager to marry her off and be rid of her as the others were. A twinge of conscience prodded her. They had raised her and wanted families of their own. It was time.

For once Rabbit Woman was not snickering, nor Pika.

Denai wondered why. She straightened her shoulders a little. "I do not want him," she said, gathering her resolve.

"Look, Denai," Trout said, and she could hear exasperation in his voice. "Look at him. The man is good to look upon, or so two of our Willow women have told me." He did not say which of the women had imparted this important information, but Denai's glance at a gaping Rabbit Woman and a wide-eyed Pika told her enough. She snorted softly to herself. No doubt it was a ploy of Rabbit Woman's to make Trout jealous.

"He is a very strong fighter," Trout continued. He patted the man's shoulder approvingly and Denai saw the stranger wince. "When we, uh, found him, he was making a spear point and I thought the point seemed to be well made. He appears to be quite skilled in stonework. No doubt he makes good knife blades and other tools, too. We have yet to see him hunt, so we

54

do not know if he is a good hunter, but we can teach him that." Trout's voice brimmed with confidence. He flicked the man's black hair. "See. We combed his hair so you would like him." He grinned. "And he has no lice."

Denai straightened a little more. "It will take more than combed hair and lack of lice to make me marry him," she said with a snarl.

Rabbit Woman stared at her. "Where did this lioness come from?" she wondered aloud. "Where is our mouse?"

Pika laughed. "I liked our mouse better."

Denai stared at the women. It was true, she marveled. For the first time since Chert's death, she felt something besides tiredness and hopelessness.

"Now, now," Uncle Rhino reproached firmly. The giggling women fell silent.

"We washed him, too," Trout assured her. He held up one of the stranger's brawny arms, still bound at the wrist. "See?"

Denai avoided the bronze face, the flashing dark eyes. The leather bonds had shrunk tight from the water, and must be hurting those wide wrists, she thought.

"And no fleas," added Trout proudly.

"Not one," Dirk confirmed.

Denai had yet to look closely at the stranger. She preferred to keep her angry gaze on her brothers—the cause of her problems.

"*Eeyak*, we took him down to the river and washed him," Flint confirmed. "He tried to get away, but we caught him again. Seems to be a good swimmer. Trout almost drowned retrieving him." Flint chuckled.

"Now that you have seen him cleaned up, I am sure

55

you will want him," Dirk spoke up. Denai gazed at her tall, usually taciturn brother. He returned her gaze with a grin. So he thought she would want this stranger, did he? His usual good sense had fled.

She surveyed her people. Rabbit Woman and Pika stared hungrily at the stranger; everyone else watched her, amusement on their faces. She shrugged, uncomfortable at the unwanted attention.

At last she took a breath and slowly pivoted in the direction of the stranger. The wind blew his thick, shoulder-length, black hair aside. His body was strong, muscular, his brown skin smooth and unmarked. She lifted her eyes to his face and found he watched her, his black eyes bright. A sneer curled his sculpted lips. Her gaze ranged over his high cheekbones and straight nose, then back to those too-bright eyes.

She flushed but held his gaze. His black eyes narrowed and she felt the heat of his glare upon her. For a heartbeat her blood pounded strangely and her breath would not come. She had not expected this. No.

Then she swallowed and her breath returned.

She closed her eyes, shutting out the sight of his handsome face with firm lips still twisted in a sneer. Plainly he did not want her. He would never want her. Nor she him. Her brothers had erred badly.

She opened her eyes and clenched her fists at her sides. Desperately she called upon her small store of courage. "I do not want him," she croaked, aware that a fragment of truth might be missing from her words.

She straightened. She had her pride. She was a woman. If she wanted a man, she would go after him.

But not this—this stranger! His contempt of her was all too evident on his handsome face.

Then, before any of her brothers could stop her, she whirled and ran back into the hut.

Chapter Four

A man laughed loudly, a grating sound in the quiet stillness.

Blade dragged his eyes away from where the woman had disappeared into the hut. The braying laugh came again, from the stout man who wore the bison horns on his head and had the bottom half of his face painted yellow. The upper half, around his eyes and forehead, was dotted in black. Heavy black braids hung down either side of his face, and he wore a small apron of ragged deerhide about his waist, unlike the other men, who wore breechcloths of leather.

An instinctive dislike swept through Blade. He could not claim to like any of the people here, but this man with the horns seemed to give off an air of cruelty, perhaps even evil.

The bison-horned man strolled forward. Blade

noted that the others moved aside. Was it out of respect or fear?

"I see that your sister is not pleased with your choice of husband." The bison-horned one snorted. "Too bad you did so much work to capture him."

The three brothers moved closer together, allies aligned against Bison-horn.

"It is not your concern, Wild Dog," said Flint, the eldest of Blade's captors.

Wild Dog smirked. "Everything about the Willow People is my concern. I am shaman and fire-keeper."

"Let us hope you are a better shaman than your father was," answered Trout.

Wild Dog whirled on him. "You will not speak about my father like that."

Trout answered calmly, "I will speak whatever I please. I have no fear of you."

"Nor do I," said Dirk, stepping forward. For a moment, Blade stood alone, forgotten in the confrontation with the shaman.

Because he was surrounded by Willow People, Blade decided to wait where he was. He was surprised to find himself curious about what these people said and did. He had been alone too long, he supposed. These were the only people he'd seen since leaving his Lion People two years before.

Fear flickered on some of the faces of the men and women in the crowd. One matron called softly to her young son and daughter, then bustled them away from the group.

Wild Dog sneered. "You are a brave man when you have your brothers beside you, are you not, Trout?"

Trout merely watched him, toying with the carved

wooden handle of his stone dagger. He said nothing.

Wild Dog looked annoyed, as though he'd failed to provoke the younger man. "Someday you will not have your brothers to back you up," said the shaman.

Blade recognized his kind. Such men tried to inspire fear in others so that they might control them.

Flint strode up to Wild Dog. "If anything happens to either of my brothers, or my sister, I will come looking for you, Wild Dog."

Blade swiftly quashed the unwilling admiration that rose in him at Flint's words. There was nothing he wanted to admire about these people. They had captured him, stolen his freedom. He could not allow himself to soften toward any of them. Not even the woman, Denai, who had seemed so defenseless.

He sidled a few steps away from the people beside him. No one noticed. They were too busy watching Wild Dog and Flint.

Wild Dog's smile at Flint was more of a grimace. He was getting his fight at last. "If anything happens to your brothers or sister, you will not know it was I, Flint. I will strike in the night. Or when your back is turned. I will use the owl. Or the magpie. Or a plant that you know nothing about. Or frog poison. I will blow a sharp, pointed stone into your brother's belly while he sleeps. You will never know it was I."

"Works of a coward," Flint said in contempt.

Wild Dog's smile disappeared. "You will regret speaking to me this way."

"I regret ever having to speak with you, Wild Dog," Flint answered.

Blade lifted a brow. Was Flint as unafraid of the shaman as he appeared? Blade thought that he would not want to cross a shaman, if he had the choice. They were powerful. He edged a few steps away from the people standing near him.

"Ayahhh!" cried Trout. He lunged for Blade and grabbed his arm.

Blade grimaced. He should have been trying to escape instead of watching these fools argue.

"He was sneaking away," Trout explained to Dirk. "Watch him."

Dirk took Blade's other arm. Blade snorted softly to himself. If he did not escape, he would soon find himself married off to their little sister.

"Ah, the unwilling husband," Wild Dog mused, turning his attention to Blade. "What makes you think he will stay with our people once he's married to your sister?"

"He will stay," Trout said confidently. "The three of us will keep him here."

Wild Dog laughed. "He does not appear to want her though, does he?"

All eyes turned to Blade. He set his jaw as best he could with a gag in his mouth and refused to acknowledge that he should care what they thought.

Trout frowned. "He will marry her."

"Your sister does not want him." Wild Dog grinned. He lifted the walking stick he carried and poked Blade in the chest with the pointed end.

A small bead of red blood appeared where the stick grazed Blade. There was a tiny obsidian shard on the end. The shaman poked the stick at Dirk and Trout, waving them away from Blade. Moving closer to Blade, he said, "I will undo his gag so that he can speak to us."

Blade felt his hair yanked sharply as the shaman fumbled with the knotted leather thong at the back of

Blade's head. Under the pretext of loosening the thong, the shaman lowered his voice, so low that only Blade could catch his words, and said, "Did you know that there is one who is stronger than you who claims the woman?"

"Wild Dog . . ." Trout said in a voice fraught with warning.

Wild Dog continued, his voice still low, "A ferocious killer bear claims the woman!"

"Wild Dog, what are you telling him?" Dirk demanded with a suspicious scowl.

Wild Dog sneered at Dirk, then turned back to Blade. The gag loosened in Blade's mouth and he spat it free.

Wild Dog whispered ominously, "The bear has already killed one man who thought he could marry her."

"What foolishness do you tell him?" Flint demanded, striding up. "Whatever it is, pay no attention to it," he instructed Blade.

Blade smirked at him. While he did not believe there was any truth to what the shaman was telling him, there was no reason for him to take his captor's side in the argument, either.

"You have said enough, Wild Dog!" said Flint.

"*Dak*, I have not said enough," Wild Dog contradicted. The shaman turned the full force of his glare on Blade and whispered, "The bear will kill Denai and any man foolish enough to marry her. Do you understand?"

Blade nodded slowly at the grimacing black-and-yellow face.

"One day the bear will return to kill Denai. If you marry her, then the bear will kill you as well."

Flint pulled Wild Dog away. "I do not know what foolishness you mutter, but it will do you no good!" he shouted.

"This shaman said something to try to scare him," protested Trout. He patted Blade's injured shoulder in a solicitous gesture. Blade would have laughed had he not already felt so angry about being captured. "We do not want him scared off," added Trout.

Wild Dog laughed. "This stranger is wise. He will know I speak the truth."

Blade knew no such thing. "I will not marry the woman," Blade said, speaking aloud for the first time.

All the Willow People stared at him in surprise except the shaman. The smirk was still on his face.

"I do not want her," Blade repeated. He turned to Flint. "I was once bound by marriage and my wife was beautiful." He sneered at Flint. "Not like your sister!"

Blade saw a muscle twitch in Flint's jaw and laughed to himself. It felt good to goad his captor. Suddenly Denai's eyes caught his. So. She had crept out of her hut, had she? He glared at her. She glared back. Blade tensed. *Good,* he thought, *it is well that she heard my words. Now she will know I do not want her either!*

"Oh, hoo, hoo," crowed Wild Dog in delight. "There! See! He does not want to marry her!"

"He will marry her." Flint's voice held a note of stubbornness that Blade did not like.

"I will not," said Blade again.

"He will die either way," Wild Dog commented slyly.

"What do you mean?" Flint asked.

"You will see." Wild Dog's smirk was most unpleasant. "For now, it is enough that I tell you that he is our enemy. We hold him by force. If we let him go he will bring his people back to seek us out in revenge and kill us."

The bright black eyes of the Willow People, glittering with mistrust, suddenly fixed on Blade.

"He must marry the woman or we will kill him in the morning!" Wild Dog ordered.

Chapter Five

Wild Dog's words rang loud in the stunned silence of the Willow People.

"Kill him?" croaked Denai.

The shaman smiled. "*Eeyak*, tomorrow morning."

The captive snorted and Denai glanced at him. He was glaring at Wild Dog, a look of disgust on his handsome face. Trout and Dirk still gripped him by either muscular arm, as if expecting him to run. And it would take two of them to hold him if he did run, she thought, eyeing his broad chest and long legs. She found herself staring at his muscled arms and flat stomach.

Her cheeks warmed. *He wants to get away from me. He does not want to marry me. He told my brothers that.*

She tossed her head defiantly, her black hair flying. *And I do not want to marry him either!*

The shaman grinned at her out of tiny, watchful

eyes. "You can be the first person to poke a burning stick into his arrogant body. I suggest you aim for his eyes, or his private parts," Wild Dog said. He did not notice Denai recoiling. "But you must wait until morning. We will let him suffer through the night."

"H-How?" Denai asked, suddenly tasting fear in her mouth.

"We will give him roasted *pisti*."

Denai's stomach knotted at his words. It was customary for the Willow People to give the leaves of the *pisti* plant to anyone who was about to die. After eating the leaves, a trance came over the dying person. Then a loved one, or sometimes a shaman, would sit with them, telling them glorious stories about the afterlife as a preparation for death. It eased a dying person's last day and gave him or her much happiness.

Unfortunately there was a much darker use for the *pisti* plant as well. It had long been known that if the thick leaves of the plant were roasted before being given to a dying person, the person then suffered from terrible hallucinations. They screamed for help from monstrous bears and rampaging lions that only they could see. Death was torturous. While the plant itself did not cause death, it did influence a person's perceptions of it, depending on how the leaves were prepared.

If Wild Dog planned to give *pisti* plant to the stranger, this man would suffer hideously throughout his last night of life.

Denai swallowed a lump of dread in her throat. She did not want to marry this stranger, but she did not want him to suffer terribly either. No creature should suffer, be it man or beast.

"And then," Wild Dog continued, "there are the shaman's tricks I can do with heated stone knives." The shaman smiled. "But we will wait until morning for that."

Denai's heart pounded. The shaman's plans were evil!

"Flint!" she cried. She ran to her older brother. "Tell them I will marry him! Tell them I will—"

"*Dak!*" cried the shaman, hurrying after her. "You said you would not!" Denai was surprised to see florid anger on his harsh, painted face. "You refused him. That means I get to kill him!"

Flint stepped protectively in front of Denai. "She wants to marry him," he told Wild Dog flatly, pushing at the shaman's chest. "He will now live! And he will be my brother by marriage," he reminded the shaman. "You are not to touch him, Wild Dog." Flint waved his brothers over.

Dirk and Trout dragged the captive over with them.

Outnumbered, the shaman spat near Flint's feet and then stalked off, shaking his stick and yelling at a little girl who played with a toy digging stick nearby. The child ran off crying for her mother.

"Denai says she will marry him," Flint announced.

"No!" snarled the captive.

Denai whirled on him. "I only do it to save you!" she cried. "Like you, I do not want this marriage!" She glared at him. "Would you rather let Wild Dog give you the *pisti* plant and play with his heated knives?"

The captive clenched his jaw, but he remained stubbornly silent.

"I thought not." She snorted, turning on her heel and stomping off to her hut.

"Good." Flint grunted. "He accepts." To his brothers he added, "Let us now prepare the marriage gifts."

* * *

The brothers tethered the stranger to a large rock while the Willow People scurried around making wedding preparations. Of necessity, these preparations would be hasty. The marriage ceremony was to take place on the morrow.

While Denai and the other women dug roots for the marriage feast, she occasionally glanced over to see her new mate sitting cross-legged in front of the rock, his jaw set mutinously, his black hair flowing back from his hawklike face while he studiously ignored the bustle going on before him.

"It is not as though I want to marry him," she muttered to herself as she dug up a wild carrot. She slapped the long, tasty root against one hand to dislodge the dirt, then popped it into her half-filled basket. She wiped at her brow with a dust-covered hand. He was still sitting there.

And what, she mused, as she tackled another carrot root, should she do about giving him the traditional wedding shirt? It was expected. No Willow bride went to her husband without giving him a wedding shirt.

She eyed him cautiously. His broad shoulders appeared even wider than Flint's, but she would give him one of Flint's shirts anyway, she decided. The new one she was making for Flint would do well. It needed but a few more beads and red quills sewn on to complete the decoration. *Eeyak*, it would probably fit, she thought, eyeing him critically.

She blushed when she saw him turn his gaze in her direction. To her mortification, he nodded his head at her and made a quick motion, as though ordering her over to him. She had walked three steps toward him before she caught herself and halted. What was she doing obeying this stranger? He had no right to call her over. Not yet.

She went back to her roots. But she could not help peeking over her shoulder now and then to see what he was doing. Once she caught his hard dark eyes glaring in her direction. She dug all the harder and ended up accidentally slashing a big carrot with her pointed digging stick. She picked up the broken pieces of carrot, scolding herself for paying so little attention to her task.

By evening, the Willow women had gathered several baskets of roots and berries. Trout had marched into camp with a fat doe over one shoulder and the decapitated head under his arm. He had skinned the carcass and gutted it. The meat would serve the wedding guests, and the head would be the center of admiration among the other wedding gifts.

Denai frowned. It should be her husband-to-be who provided the deer, not her own kinsman, but she guessed her brothers knew her surly bridegroom would not hunt anything for the wedding. He would rather run away. She shook her head, angry with herself for wanting him to hunt the deer. It was only natural that he would want to run away. She would, too, if she were being forced into a marriage.

She carried the loaded basket over to her brush hut and set it down outside the open doorway. Not far away, her brothers had built their own brush shelters. She saw Dirk and Trout each tying one of their captive's legs to stout stakes driven into the ground.

How humiliated he must feel, she thought to herself, yet he looked more angry than humiliated. In fact, she realized, he looked furious. He kicked out at Dirk and Dirk grabbed his foot. She heard her brother warn him in a low voice not to kick again.

Denai shrugged off her pity at his humiliation. Death was far worse than humiliation, and death was what he would face if she did not marry him. Best not to spare any pity for him! She should keep it for herself. She was also being forced to marry!

She stoked up the dying embers in the hearth outside her hut. Once she had the small fire rekindled, she pretended to enter her home, but instead she lingered inside the doorway, where he could not see her. Now she had a better view of him. She felt a shiver as she admired his muscular frame, his piercing eyes. He was magnificent. . . .

Her hands flew to her face. What was she doing, thinking such thoughts?

She should not be. She was marrying the man to save his life, not to share his bed! She ducked farther inside her hut.

She remembered how he had nodded his head at her. What had he wanted from her? she wondered uneasily.

She must prepare for the wedding, not think about the man staked out close to her door. Denai crawled across the rushes of her floor and pawed through her clothing until she found what she was looking for: the almost finished shirt for Flint. Now it would be for him. Her new husband. Husband. How strange the thought.

She held the shirt up, eyeing it critically in the waning light. Would it fit? She decided it would and dragged her small basket of quills and beads over. She must finish it before the night was through.

She sat sewing by the fire's flickering light until she could no longer see anything. At last the shirt was finished. She was about to lie down on her reed mats when she heard a familiar voice outside her hut.

"Denai!"

She groaned. "What do you want, Rabbit Woman?" Slowly Denai rose and staggered out of her hut. As usual, Pika accompanied Rabbit Woman.

They both giggled in reply. Rabbit Woman held up a beautiful doeskin dress. Denai gasped. By firelight she could see a simple yoke of red and blue quills sewn around the neckline. The dress, the color of sand, showed exquisite workmanship. Denai could not stop herself from reaching out to touch the soft, smooth hide.

"Oh, it is beautiful," she murmured. Then she glanced at Rabbit Woman. "Why—why are you showing me this?"

Rabbit Woman smiled innocently. "It is for you to wear on your wedding day. I am happy you are to be wed at last."

Denai could well believe that. "Now Trout will be free to marry," Denai muttered.

Pika giggled and Denai wished she had not spoken her thought aloud. "But it is beautiful," Denai protested. "Surely you do not mean to give it to me."

"*Dak, dak,*" Rabbit Woman answered hastily. "I do not give it to you. I but loan it."

Denai nodded and tried to ignore the disappointment that welled inside her. She stroked the soft material. "I will be happy to wear it," she answered Rabbit Woman. "Thank you."

Rabbit Woman would not meet her eyes. "It is naught," she answered quietly. Pika giggled. Rabbit Woman raised her dark eyes. "Perhaps you will tell Trout that I lent you the dress?"

Ah, thought Denai. *So that is why she is being kind to me. She wants Trout to know.* "Eeyak," Denai answered aloud. "I will tell him."

Rabbit Woman's smile looked satisfied.

Some of the joy went out of Denai. She had been foolish to hope this was a kindness from Rabbit Woman.

"Perhaps we will be sisters by marriage someday," said Rabbit Woman.

"Perhaps," answered Denai, though she doubted it. Trout had never appeared very interested in Rabbit Woman. Perhaps Rabbit Woman was getting desperate.

Denai peered at the shorter woman but could read nothing in her hard but pretty features.

"Thank you for the dress," Denai said softly, clutching the dress. She turned to enter her hut.

"May you sleep well," Rabbit Woman answered politely. Pika giggled and the two women left.

Denai set the dress aside and lay down. *How unusual for Rabbit Woman to be so kind,* she thought uneasily. *How unusual.*

But she could not sleep. She kept thinking about the captive, about his long hair, his rugged face, his strong body. He had seemed so angry with his capture. As any man would, she realized. Or woman.

Added to this, he must be furious about being forced to marry, too, she thought guiltily. She sat up. She should not feel guilty, she scolded herself. She was saving his life! If she did not marry him, he would die in the morning.

She straightened the bed furs on the mats. What was it he had wanted of her? Curious now, she knew she could not sleep until she found out. Perhaps he was thirsty, she thought. How long had it been since her brothers had let him drink or eat?

Taking a large deer bladder of water and some smoked meat from a basket, she crept out of the hut.

She tiptoed past her brothers' huts to where the stranger lay. He was staked out on his back, legs and arms tied. He was asleep. She watched the even rise and fall of his broad chest. *I should not be here. . . .* She had turned around to sneak back into her hut when his low voice stopped her.

"Come here," he said.

She whirled, her heart pounding. She should go back to her hut; she should not be here with him. Her brothers would be furious.

"Come here," he said again.

His low voice drew her, and she found herself taking several steps closer to him before she stopped herself. "What—what is it you wanted of me? You signaled me to come to you this afternoon. Over by the rock."

He did not answer. She remembered she was holding the water bladder and the meat. She took a step closer. "Are you hungry?"

"*Eeyak.* Your brothers do not think to feed me."

Denai flushed and was glad of the night's dark cover to hide her embarrassment from him. Her brothers could be forgetful at times.

She crept closer until she could almost touch him. "I brought you some food. Water, too."

When he did not say anything, she knelt down beside him. "I will give you the water first," she murmured. She lifted the bladder and dribbled water into his mouth. But the dribble became a torrent and his mouth filled and he choked and coughed.

She waited, writhing inwardly at her clumsiness.

73

She must remember to pour slowly. When he was done choking and gasping she asked timidly, "Meat?"

"*Eeyak,* but do not stuff it in my mouth. If I choke on that I will not live until morning. And then you will have no husband."

She thought she heard a trace of humor in his voice, but what he said was not funny at all.

"I do not need a husband," she said stiffly. Indeed, she did not expect one. Had not for a long time. Not since the short-faced bear accident. That this stranger was to be her husband still seemed . . . odd, yes, that was it. Odd. As though it would not truly happen. "They would have killed you if I had not agreed to marry you. You know that."

"Ah. So now you are saving my life." His voice held a note of anger this time.

"*Eeyak.* I *am* saving your life." Stubborn man! So he did not like that. Well, too bad. She would not have another man's death on her conscience. Chert's was enough. If she could prevent a man's death, and this time she could, then, by the Great Mother, she would!

"More water?" she asked.

"*Dak,* no!" His voice was harsh. He turned his face away from her and she had the sudden feeling she had been dismissed.

She fidgeted. "Why did you call me over during the heat of the day?" she asked at last.

He turned back to face her, shifting position a little. Having one's limbs tied to stakes must be uncomfortable, she thought. Perhaps she should ask Trout if he would untie—

"I thought you should know my name."

She started. "You would tell me?"

He laughed harshly. "I might. If you promise to go away, back to your hut."

She flushed, and her grip on the water bladder tightened. "I do not find you amusing," she said.

"Good. I do not find you amusing either," he answered.

"I find you to be a bother," she continued.

"Oh, Great Mother!" He snorted.

"And I find your prayers rude."

"Will you just go?" He turned his head away from her again and suddenly she wanted to pour the remaining water over his head. She turned the bladder upside down and water began to pour.

He gave a squawk and closed his eyes. "Aeeyah! Stop that!"

"I will not," she said calmly. *Insufferable man!* She squeezed the bladder a little harder and more water came out. On his nose, this time.

He sputtered. "You fool!" he cried. "Take that thing away."

"No!" More water dribbled out, this time on his mouth, his chin, back to his eyes.

"I do not want to marry you," he snarled. "You do not even tempt me! My first wife looked better than you! You are plain and no man wants you! No man wants you!"

She squeezed the last dribble of water onto his face and ignored the tears pouring down her cheeks. "I do not want to marry you either, you horrible man!" she cried. She flung the bladder aside and raced back to her hut.

Her hands shook, she was so angry. "Horrible man!" she muttered to the dark interior of her hut. "Horrible! Worse than a short-faced bear!" Even now his contemptuous words rang in her ears and she clapped her hands over them to keep out the memory of his voice. *No man wants you!*

She gritted her teeth. It was going to be a miserable marriage, she just knew it.

And she still did not know his name.

Chapter Six

When they untied his wrists, the blood coursed through Blade's veins and into his hands and fingers. He gritted his teeth against the pain. Trout untied the leather bonds on Blade's feet. Now his feet throbbed, too.

He swayed a little, striving to keep his balance. It would not do for the groom to keel over onto the ground, he thought grimly, no matter how badly he ached. At least his shoulder had healed.

"There," Trout said in satisfaction. "You are all untied." He rose and met Blade's eyes. The Willow man's eyes flashed. "Do not attempt to run away, stranger. My brothers and I will chase you down. You will marry my sister."

Blade snorted his disgust. "I do not want your sister."

Flint came up to them just in time to hear Blade's

words. "You may not want her, but you are going to marry her! And you are going to treat her well."

"And if I do not?" Blade demanded sullenly.

"Hunting accidents have been known to happen," answered Flint enigmatically.

Blade did not like his words. He glared at Flint, trying to determine if the Willow man was bluffing. Flint's face was as impassive as stone. "Why do you marry off your sister to someone who does not want her?" Blade asked at last. "Do you hate her?"

"Dak," answered Flint shortly. Blade waited, but the Willow man did not explain further.

"Flint! Trout!" Turtle, a stout, middle-aged Willow man, came running up. "We need to know what other meats you have to offer. The women are complaining that there is not enough meat!"

"Not enough meat?" Trout exclaimed. "Why, I killed two deer yesterday. Dirk caught seven fish. And Flint, you snared all those sage hens. What are they talking about, not enough meat? There should be plenty!"

Turtle shook his head. "You come and tell them." Excited, the two brothers hurried away with him to sort out the dilemma, leaving Blade, for a moment, untended.

Blade smiled slyly to himself and surveyed the camp. Some women were cleaning roots in the stream, others were stoking a fire, and another group was setting wedding gifts onto a large woven mat. In the center of the mat was a deer head. The men sat around in groups, talking and sharpening their stone tools. Now and then one of the men would wander over to advise the women on how best to stoke the fire where the roots were baking. Then he would be chased away for his efforts.

Behind the camp and across a dirt-and-sagebrush field grew a small forest of pine. If Blade could make it to the pines, he could escape these fools.

He backed away, careful to listen for any warning cry that he had been spotted. No one noticed.

Flint and Trout were busy waving their arms at some Willow women on one side of a fire who were busy waving their arms back at the men. Dirk was nowhere to be seen.

Blade whirled and ran. He was halfway to the pine trees when a cry went up. He glanced over one shoulder. It was Dirk, pointing at Blade and shouting something to his brothers. The three raced after the fleeing bridegroom.

Now pursued, Blade ran harder. The dirt ground passed under his feet in a brown blur. He had almost reached the pines when someone grabbed his legs from behind and he went tumbling to the ground. Wincing, Blade struggled to get Dirk off him before the other two reached them. But the thin man had a wiry strength, and he battled Blade until his brothers joined him. Flint and Trout dragged Blade and Dirk apart.

Panting, Blade was pushed, prodded and dragged, wrists bound once more, back to the encampment. Several of the women glared at him as he walked past them. "Your Willow women do not seem to like it that the groom tried to run away on his wedding day," Blade commented with a smirk.

"Stay quiet," Trout ordered. Even this generally good-natured man appeared angry for a change.

Flint growled at him. "You will not shame my family again. You will marry my sister and that will be that!"

"I do not want your sister!"

79

Flint only shrugged his shoulders indifferently at this information. He tied Blade's feet. When Blade was hobbled so that he could take only small steps, Flint observed firmly, "Now you are well tied."

Blade subtly tested the bindings and found Flint's words to be true. He would not be running away again.

"Take him over to where the wedding gifts are," Flint ordered Dirk. "It is time for the marriage to take place." To Trout he said, "Get Denai and Uncle Rhino. It is time."

While Trout was fetching the bride, Blade was led to the woven mat where the gifts were set out. He glanced down at the spears and shirt and baskets of food and he sniffed in contempt. Truth to tell, there were almost as many gifts here as on the day he had married Amethyst, but he would not let these people know that. He glared at those watching him.

"Sit down," Dirk ordered. When Blade refused, Dirk kicked Blade's feet out from under him. Blade landed heavily. Dirk squatted down to eye level.

"My brothers and I," Dirk said slowly, "expect that you will be a good husband to my sister." His glare pinned Blade. Dirk fingered one of the spears, usually a gift that the groom would present to the bride's family. Blade noticed that the stonework along the edges of the spear points was very well executed.

"You have a choice ahead of you," Dirk continued softly. "You can live with my sister and do your best to treat her well, and you can join my brothers and me in our hunting group, or you can treat her poorly. If you do that"—Dirk's tone was positively menacing—"you will not live long. Do you understand?"

Blade glared back. This was his second warning

from one of Denai's brothers. It did not appear that they hated her; rather they seemed to be most concerned about her and her safety. He wondered if he had been misled about her value to the Willow People.

"I understand," Blade answered coolly. He would show no fear to Dirk. Nor Flint.

"Good," Dirk said. "I want my sister to be happy."

Then why marry her off to a stranger? Blade wanted to ask, but the sudden vulnerability in the other man's eyes stilled his tongue. *Her brothers care for her*, he realized suddenly. Then, hard on that thought, *They must be desperate.*

The old headman—Uncle Rhino, Flint called him—ducked out of his brush hut and walked over to where the wedding gifts were laid out. He looked suitably imposing for the occasion, Blade thought. He was dressed in a salmon-skin vest and three heavy stone necklaces, as well as his usual sagebark sandals. Today he wore a sagebark apron and on his head he wore a double-peaked cap of blue jay feathers. Blue jay feathers adorned his ankles.

But he was no match for the bride. She wore a sand-colored, knee-length doeskin dress with red and blue quills, and her shining black hair hung loose around her face. On top of her head she wore the delicate marriage cap; interlaced white and blue stone beads formed a light covering for her head. Some of the beads dangled along her forehead. Henceforth she was entitled to wear the cap as befitted a married woman.

Trout guided her over to where the gifts were. Blade watched her, but she studiously avoided his gaze.

He smiled to himself. She looked rather pretty, and he wondered why none of the Willow men had seen

81

that for himself. Indeed, now he could see glances and hear murmurings among the Willow men—and women—and he thought they seemed rather surprised at Denai's newly discovered beauty.

Two giggling young women hurried over to Denai. "Oh, Denai, you look lovely," exclaimed one, pressing her hand into Denai's back. Blade was surprised to see Denai wince. She quickly stepped away from the two women. Had she been hurt?

She straightened, trying to recover her composure. The two women walked away, giggling.

He wondered idly what they had done to his bride to make her wince.

"Bring the groom," Uncle Rhino ordered, and Blade was shoved forward. He stumbled, due to the hobbles on his ankles, but Trout caught him before he fell. Blade managed to regain his balance and Trout pushed him, shuffling, over to where Denai awaited.

Uncle Rhino lifted a hand and the drumming began. Several old men and women tapped sticks on decorated drums. They sang a song in time to the drums, their voices rising and falling in rhythm with their drumming. Then a shy young girl stepped forward and sang a wedding song. The audience listened and murmured appreciatively when she was done. Uncle Rhino handed her a basket of roots to thank her for her song. Her proud parents led her away to the edge of the crowd.

Blade yawned, pretending boredom, though truly the girl had sung very well. He did not want these Willow People to know he approved of any part of this wretched event.

The audience importuned a young man, his hair in four braids down his back, to come forward and sing a song. Uncle Rhino held up a chunk of green stone, big enough to be made into a fine spear point, to further entice the young man forward. Two other young men separated from the crowd and, grinning, tussled with the braided man and finally pushed him over to Uncle Rhino. The old headman cajoled him in a low voice, and finally the young man consented to sing.

His voice, too, was very good. At the end of the song, he happily received his gift of the green stone and took his place at the edge of the crowd.

After the singing, Uncle Rhino burned some branches of sage in a small fire. While the smoke hovered in the air, he chanted, "This man will hunt meat for his wife."

The Willow People responded, "*Eeyak*, it is good."

"This man will treat his wife with kindness."

"*Eeyak*, it is good."

"This woman will bear her husband's children."

"*Eeyak*, it is good."

"This woman will treat her husband with kindness."

"*Eeyak*, it is good."

Uncle Rhino spoke further about the groom's duties to the bride and the bride's duties to the groom. When the fire died down, Uncle Rhino gave three high-pitched yelps and everyone fell silent.

The silence lasted for several minutes as the headman stood with his arms raised to the sky and his eyes closed. He sang a song under his breath, but Blade could only catch a few words. They had to do with hope for a good marriage.

Blade glanced away from the chanting headman. He did not want to have anything to do with this marriage, and hope for it was the last thing he wanted. When he could escape, he would!

His glance skidded to the bride. He watched her staring at the headman, then, feeling his eyes upon her, she lifted her eyes to meet his. Was that a tiny smile on her lips? Was that hope in her dark, dark eyes?

His fists clenched and his eyes narrowed. She had hope, did she? Hope that this false marriage would in some way prove true? Angrily, he pulled his wrists, trying to break the bonds that held him. *Look at me,* he wanted to shout. *I am forced to marry you. Whatever we have between us, it will not be true!*

Helpless and angry, he glanced away from her. He would not be part of this false marriage. It took more than gifts and songs and words and sage smoke to make a true marriage.

He thought briefly of Amethyst. *Eeyak,* it took honesty and love . . . and faithfulness. *Dak,* he would not encourage this maiden of the Willow People, for he would leave her as soon as he could.

The crowd surged around Uncle Rhino and the bride. They commented on the bulging baskets of roots and vegetables and exclaimed over the spears. Finally, the bride picked up a leather shirt that lay among the gifts. She walked over to Blade and held it up in front of him.

"This is my wedding gift to you," she murmured.

He glared at the shirt, summoning saliva in his mouth. He would spit on the shirt to show his contempt of the marriage and these people. But when Denai lowered the beautifully beaded shirt a little and peeked over at him, her dark eyes shining, he found he could not shame her so in front of her people. He swallowed his saliva and stared at her instead.

He refused to acknowledge the shirt; that much he could do.

Trout stepped forward, a cougar head and skin draped over him to disguise himself. He held a spear in each hand. He announced, "Today I am a kinsman of the groom, not of the bride! I will prove that I am a kinsman of the groom!" He stalked around in a small circle in front of the Willow People and scowled at each of them. Some he pretended to lunge at.

Squirming, Blade realized that Trout was imitating Blade's own behavior since his capture. It seemed to the snickering Willow People that all he had done since his capture was scowl.

Then Trout lifted the spears and shook them. He broke into a whirling, gyrating dance, brandishing the spears with ferocity.

The crowd murmured happily at his antics. Suddenly Trout dashed off as though to run away from the wedding. Flint and Dirk went after him and brought him back, kicking and flailing his arms.

Blade snorted. The Willow People howled with laughter. Everyone recognized Blade's constant attempts at escape. Even Blade could not keep a small smile from creeping to his lips.

Trout shook the spears again. "These spears," he told the crowd, "are a gift to the bride's family! They will be used to hunt meat for her and for everyone in her family! As kinsman to the groom, I promise such!"

Blade clenched his jaw. No one could make a promise on his behalf, no one! He had no people, and Trout was no kinsman. These people were fools!

Now Trout was pointing to the deer's head that graced the woven mat of gifts. "As kinsman of the groom, I have provided meat for this wedding feast.

This fat deer shows that the groom is a good hunter, strong and sure, and able to provide meat for his bride and her children. They will never go hungry," Trout boasted, shaking the spears for emphasis.

While the appreciative Willow People were nudging each other and murmuring over Trout's words, Trout's eyes flashed at Blade, warning him that he must indeed provide meat. Blade glared back at Trout.

Flint strode up to Blade and undid his leather bonds at the wrist with one slice of his sharp obsidian knife. Dirk undid the bonds on Blade's ankles.

Blade shook his wrists and kicked his feet to get the blood flowing. Then he folded his arms across his chest. Defiantly.

"You are now married into the Willow People," Flint stated solemnly. "Your blood will be our blood, your people our people. Your children will grow strong with us."

Blade glared at him, wondering if Flint spoke the truth. Would he have children? Would they be raised with these Willow People? *No!* he warned himself. *This is their doing. They want me to believe this. I will not. I will escape.* He glared at the bride. *I did not choose her. I do not want her!*

Flint and Dirk stepped away, leaving Blade free. Trout did a little dance, then shuffled off to his brush hut. When he returned moments later, it was in his usual leather breechcloth.

"No longer my kinsman?" taunted Blade.

Trout laughed. "*Eeyak*, but by marriage now." His words reminded Blade of his bride. He glanced around, looking for Denai. Did she think this ceremony had changed everything?

He saw her talking with some women, and when she

saw him looking at her she walked over, her dark eyes holding his.

He watched her come steadily onward, her steps confident. She smiled up at him when she reached him.

"You seem very happy for a woman forced into marriage," he observed.

She chuckled. "It brings satisfaction to save a man's life," she answered. She kept smiling at the other Willow People, as though the words they spoke were not spear points pricking one another.

He scowled at her.

Drums began pounding, heavy drums, dance drums. The Willow People hooted and laughed and began shuffling in a large circle in time to the drumming.

"I would like to dance on this day. Would you?" his new bride bravely asked.

"*Dak.*"

"Do you not wish to celebrate your marriage?"

"This is a false marriage," he pronounced. "I have been forced to marry you."

"And I you," she snapped, irritated. Her dark eyes were bright with unshed tears. "I am saving your worthless life!"

Chastened, he glanced away, as though studying the dancers. Guilt pricked Blade as he thought that if the shaman had had his way, Blade would be dead by now. "Where is the shaman?" he asked.

"Sulking in his hut," she answered. "He wanted you killed. Remember?"

Blade nodded. She stood watching the dancers, looking unhappy in her quill-decorated bridal dress. He put his hand low on her back and saw her wince. "Does my touch hurt you?" he asked.

"*Dak*, it is not that," she said. She reddened.

"What is it, then?"

She hesitated, then blurted, "I borrowed this dress from—from a friend. I thought she was a friend," Denai amended. "She stuck sharp tips of porcupine quill in the back, pointing inward, so that when I wore the dress I would get scraped. The quills do not show on the outside, and I did not know she had done this until I had put the dress on." Denai stared miserably at the ground.

Blade's jaw clenched, but he said nothing. Her pain was no concern of his.

He surveyed the shuffling, drumming Willow People and wondered when he should escape. He spotted the leather shirt she had made for him. "Are there any quills in that shirt you made for me?" he asked.

She glanced at him askance. "Why, a few. For decoration. B-but only on the outside."

"I am most relieved to hear that," he answered.

Her gaze was uncertain as she ventured, "I suppose I could sew a few quill points into the back of the shirt if you do not go hunting meat often enough to please me."

Blade gave her a sharp glance.

She was watching him, blushing, but with a tiny smile.

Surprised at her joking answer, he could only stare.

"Let us dance," she said again and took his hand and led him into the line of dancers.

"I do not want to dance," he said stubbornly.

"Move your feet," she ordered.

He set his jaw, but did as she said. When the beat changed, he took her hand and led her away from the dancers. He ignored Flint and Dirk's wary appraisals.

Denai's heart pounded. Where was he leading her? The grip of her new husband was proving formidable. She could not withdraw her hand from his tight grasp. She hurried along after him.

He does not want me, she told herself. *He told me before that he does not want me.* But she felt warm inside when she thought about how they had shared a small joke. *Perhaps he will grow to like me,* she thought, a tiny bud of hope unfurling in her heart. *Perhaps he will want to stay with me. And have children . . .*

The very audacity of her thoughts left her wordless as she hurried after him.

They found a place a little away from the dancers, but still within sight of Flint and Dirk. Knowing that her brothers could see her, and would come to her aid if she needed them, made Denai feel more confident.

Finally her new husband halted. He let go of her hand quickly.

"You must understand this," he said, his dark eyes fierce as he stared into hers. "I do not want a wife. I do not want you. I have been forced to marry you, but as soon as I can, I will escape you and your people!"

Chapter Seven

Denai narrowed her eyes. "I know you did not want to marry me." She snarled. "I never thought you did."

"I see that you understand—" Blade began.

"I understand," she cut in. "But it seems that we are married. Whether you want it or not!"

That silenced him.

"And whether I want it or not," she added sadly.

He stared at her for a moment. "Do not think to gain my pity," he said disdainfully.

"Pity!" she cried. "I do not want your pity!" Why did her new husband jerk as if startled by her words? "I do not want anything from you," she finished.

"Then why—"

"Why did I marry you? To save your life! Ah, but I see that you do not believe me."

He glared at her, arms across his chest, dark eyes alight with battle.

"I suppose you were such a fine man among your people, and so many maidens sought you out that you expect all women to want you?"

His lips tightened. He looked angry, but he said nothing.

Glaring at his handsome face, she could well believe that women had sought him out. She had seen the way that Rabbit Woman and Pika had looked at him. Her cheeks flushed as she cried, "Tell me, did they seek you out? Tell me!" Now why did she speak to him so? Perhaps it was because no one sought her out, not one of the Willow men—she who was unwanted by men. "Who are your people?" she asked angrily.

He shook his head, refusing to tell her.

Her anger subsided a little, and she prodded, "You do have people, do you not?"

"*Dak,* I do not."

She stared at him in disbelief. "Everyone has people. Everyone comes from somewhere."

"I do not."

Taken aback, she stared at him. "Once you were going to tell me your name," she whispered.

He laughed harshly. "You are mistaken. I never intended to tell you anything."

But he lied; she knew he did. He had intended to tell her his name; he had told her so yesterday when she'd brought him the water and meat. She glared at him, this new husband of hers. How was she going to weave a life with this man? Then swiftly she remembered: she was not going to weave a life with him. She had only married him to save him. There had been no agreement about a true marriage between them. Yet that was what she found herself wanting. She flushed in embarrassment. What a fool she was!

"Denai," Flint said, coming up to them. Dirk and Trout were with him. "Your brothers and I wish to talk with you about your new husband."

She shrugged her shoulders. "Very well. Talk."

"Alone," he said, eyeing her new husband.

She glanced at her waiting brothers, then at him. Shrugging, she moved away. "What is it you have to tell me?"

"Denai, your brothers and I do not yet trust this man. We do not think we can leave you alone with him."

"Does he have a name?" she asked Flint.

Flint shook his head. "No name that we learned."

"He says he has no people, either," she observed.

"No people?" said Trout in amazement. "Why, everyone has people."

"He says he does not." All four Willow siblings stared at Denai's new husband.

"That is odd," commented Dirk.

"He lies, no doubt," Flint said reasonably. "He came from somewhere. He even mentioned a wife before."

Denai flushed. "I wonder if she still lives, if he wants to go back to her?"

Silence greeted this remark.

"He was alone when we found him," Dirk said. "He had no wife with him then."

"We will keep him with us," Flint said firmly. "He is yours, Denai."

Her brother's words were strangely reassuring. She smiled at Flint, but said nothing. A little mouse of guilt was gnawing at her. Perhaps that was why he was so insistent that he would escape. He already had a wife.

She found she did not like that thought. *I must ask him,* she thought. *Soon.*

"Denai," Flint continued, "because we do not trust this man yet, we will continue to stay with you and with him until we are satisfied that he means you no harm."

She glanced at her husband and shivered. If he meant her harm, he would be deadly, she thought.

"Very well," she answered. "What are you going to do?"

"This is our plan," Flint said. "We will take him back to where we first captured him. He has some things there, some spear points, some other tools. Things he will want. It will take a day or more. We will learn more about him on the way there."

"*Eeyak*," Trout added. "We will learn if he can be trusted with you."

Denai thought about her brothers' words. "What if he cannot be trusted?"

"We will take care of that," Dirk said calmly.

"You would not kill him?" she begged.

All three brothers stared at Denai. She saw the surprise on Dirk's and Trout's faces.

"I think," Flint said slowly, "that our sister likes her new mate."

She blushed.

"We will not kill him," Flint promised.

She let out a breath.

"Unless we have to."

She glanced at her new husband, then back at Flint. "I will come with you."

"*Dak*," Flint said. "It will be too dangerous."

She faced her eldest brother. "I care not about the danger. I will come. He is my husband."

Trout was busy staring at the ground. Dirk was humming and glancing at the sky. Clearly neither one of them wanted to get into the argument between siblings.

"I will come with you, Flint," she repeated slowly, steadily.

Flint sighed. "You are a stubborn woman."

She smiled, sensing victory. "*Eeyak,* I am."

"Very well, you will come with us," Flint conceded.

Her smile broadened. "My husband needs a name," she said.

"Name him then," replied Flint. "Tell him we leave before nightfall."

They had been traveling for two days and had finally reached the top of the hill where Blade had been captured. His weapons and stones were still there, he saw, though the leather bag that he carried food in had a big hole chewed through it, probably by mice, and the meat was gone. But his spear points were there, and—Great Mother!—so was the piece of obsidian that had belonged to his great-grandfather.

He picked up the obsidian. For this alone he should be grateful that the Willow men had allowed him to return, he supposed. But he did not feel grateful. He felt angry all over again at his captors.

The stone warmed in his hand. The trip had been rather leisurely; the brothers had ambled along. They seemed in no hurry. They had joked and laughed among each other and occasionally had included him.

He had ignored them. All he wanted was to get away from these people.

Denai was looking off to the south. Her black hair blew back from her face and he saw the pensive look in her eyes. To his surprise she had proved to be an able traveling companion, good-natured with her brothers, and carrying her share willingly. And every meal she prepared was delicious. *Dak*, he corrected himself. It was not delicious. It was . . . adequate. That was it. Her cooking was nothing special. And neither was she. He must remember that.

She must have felt his eyes upon her. She swung to face him and smiled shyly.

He glanced away, ignoring the pang in his heart. He did not want her to like him. He did not want to like her. He did not want her. He did not want another woman. Ever. Amethyst had caused him enough pain for a lifetime. He needed no more.

Denai walked over to him, the gravel underfoot crunching with each step. "Antelope," she said to Blade, "do you have all your possessions now?" She eyed the beautiful piece of obsidian in his hand but said nothing.

He closed his hand over it, as if protecting it from her gaze. "*Eeyak*, I have all my possessions."

"Good. We will head back to our people soon."

"Tomorrow," Flint confirmed. "It is too late in the day to start out now. We will camp here for the night."

By now Blade had learned that Flint was the leader and the others did as he told them. Occasionally Denai or one of the other brothers would change an order, but they usually followed what Flint said. It made for an easy working arrangement.

Flint sauntered away.

Blade turned to Denai. "My name," he said distinctly, "is not Antelope."

She put her hand up to screen the lowering sun from her eyes. "It is the name I have given you."

"It is not my name."

"If you would tell me your name, then I would call

95

you by your name." She shrugged. "But as you do not, I must call you Antelope."

He gritted his teeth. "My name is Blade."

She gave a tiny smile—one he recognized. It was the smile that told him she had just received whatever it was she wanted. She smiled it often around her indulgent brothers.

"Thank you, Blade," she said softly.

He glanced away to the south, wishing now he had not told her his name. "Look." He pointed. "A mammoth herd."

She looked to where he indicated. "Seven of them," she cried. "And a baby!"

The mammoth herd looked tiny in the far distance. Their sand-colored, woolly coats blended in with the brown, sage-covered desert, and it took sharp eyes to spot them. The herd browsed on clumps of grass. Denai had to have good eyesight to see the mammoth calf.

They gazed at the mammoths. It had been a long time since he had hunted mammoths. To hunt the giant animals a man needed to have other men who would hunt with him as partners.

Denai seemed entranced by the mammoths. *Her brothers would be good hunting partners,* he thought. *Knowledgeable and skilled.*

He tore his gaze away from her. He did not want her for a wife, nor her brothers for hunting partners.

"Blade?"

Something must have scared the herd, for they were moving now, the lead matriarch waving her trunk. From this distance he could not hear her trumpet, but from her actions Blade guessed that she was warning the herd of danger. He surveyed the terrain around the herd. Perhaps a lion was creeping up on them. . . .

"What is it?" he asked, his eyes on the mammoths.

"Did—did you leave a wife behind?"

He watched the calf. It was in the greatest danger, being the youngest and weakest. But the other mammoths were circling around it, the mother in the middle with it, protecting it. Whatever the threat, lion or saber-toothed cat, it would have to get past that circle of powerful trunks and feet.

"*Dak.*"

She glanced at him then, the wind on the hilltop blowing her hair over her face so he could not read her eyes. His gaze swung back to the herd.

"But you had a wife?"

It was a saber-tooth. He could see the big cat creeping along the sand-colored gravel, the black stripes on its back the only visible signs of its movement. He wished he was down there, hunting the mammoths, hunting the saber-tooth.

"Once."

"You said she was beautiful. I heard you tell my brothers that."

He did not answer.

"What happened to her?" Denai asked.

"She died."

There was only the wind, whipping her hair back and whistling in his ears. The saber-tooth made its charge. It tried to get past the matriarch to the tender calf. But the huge elephant gored the saber-tooth in the stomach, her tusks bloody as she tossed the cat. The saber-tooth landed, sprawling, clawing the ground, churning, twisting, awkward in its death.

The cat's carcass was trampled under the pounding forefeet of the angry matriarch. She trumpeted her triumph and flapped her ears. Life could be hard in this land.

"The man I was betrothed to marry also died," Denai volunteered. He was surprised to hear her tell him that. Then he realized she was telling him something more: she knew what it was like to lose a mate to death.

He clenched his hand around the hard obsidian rock. He did not want to hear about her pain. He did not want to tell her his.

But the words came out. "She drowned. I could not help her."

It was the first time he had told anyone about Amethyst—anyone, since her death. The first time he had said aloud what was in his heart. His helplessness.

Denai met his eyes and he saw her tears. For him.

His grip on the stone was so tight he cut his finger on one sharp edge. He ignored the blood. "I do not want another woman. Ever!"

"You loved her so much then?" she murmured.

He snorted his disgust and glanced away, searching the horizon for the mammoth herd. They had wandered away from the saber-tooth carcass and were browsing once again.

"I hated her." *And loved her,* he added silently, trying to push the painful memories from his mind.

Denai's brown eyes were wide in disbelief.

Let her think what she likes. I care not, he told himself. He stared at the dead cat.

The woman beside him was silent. "I did not hate Chert," she said. "I loved him." She bowed her head and he saw her body tremble. It could have been the strong wind on the hill that he heard. Or it could have been sobs.

"I loved my wife, too," he admitted softly. But she kept sobbing and he thought she did not hear him.

"How can you love someone and hate them as well?" she asked, wiping at her eyes.

He shook his head. "I do not know," he admitted. "But that is how I feel."

"Is that why you did not want to marry?" The woman was cunning, he thought. She had hit unerringly upon the truth.

"I did not want to marry," he answered stubbornly. "I did not want to marry you."

She flinched. "I did not want to marry you either," she replied, and her voice took on the cold of the wind. "I only married you to save your life! I see now that I should have let you die! You are ungrateful."

He snorted.

She was angry. He could see it in her flashing dark eyes. "You are free to go! Free to run away. I do not want you either!" she cried.

He stared at the mammoth herd. So she was giving him his freedom, was she? he mused. He could go down there, down to the mammoth herd, follow them for as long as he liked, camp wherever he wanted. He would be free to live his life as he had the past two years. Alone.

After a while he asked, "What about the bear?"

"What bear?" she cried. "What are you talking about?"

"The short-faced bear," he said calmly. "The bear that the shaman said is going to come back and kill you."

Her eyes were wild. "I do not know anything about a short-faced bear! What—When . . . ?"

She looked so bewildered that he almost believed

her. Almost. "The shaman told me that the bear that killed Chert was going to come back and kill you. And whoever you took as mate."

She stared at him, her eyes round. "The shaman said that?"

Blade glanced over to where her brothers were building a small fire on the lee side of the hill, sheltered from the wind. "Ask your brothers. They must know this."

"Flint! Trout! Dirk!" she called.

They looked up from their work and sauntered over.

"This man, Blade, tells me that the shaman told him the short-faced bear that killed Chert is supposed to return and kill me! Has Wild Dog said such a thing to you?"

Trout and Flint shook their heads. Dirk frowned.

"Blade says that the shaman said the short-faced bear will kill any man who chooses me as a mate." She looked affronted.

Flint frowned. "I have long suspected that Wild Dog was telling lies about you. We knew he blamed you for Chert's death. But there always seemed to be something more. I could never get anyone to tell me what he said."

"The Willow men are afraid of you, Denai," Trout said, "afraid to marry you. We, your brothers, knew something was wrong, but we did not know what it was."

"They are afraid of the bear," she mused. She shook her head. "Wild Dog has said very bad things about me." She looked ready to cry.

Trout put an arm around her. She bowed her black head.

All four Willow People remained silent for a time.

"That is why no man would offer for her," said Dirk at last. "They were afraid to fight the bear."

Three pairs of masculine eyes studied Blade. Finally Flint said, "You knew this, Blade, and yet you married her?"

"I had little choice," Blade replied contemptuously. "Remember?"

Flint looked chagrined. His brothers looked embarrassed. "Let us finish building the fire," Dirk said. Trout released Denai, and the brothers returned to the lee side of the hill.

Denai remained silent, her eyes focused on the now lounging mammoth herd. The matriarch sprayed dust over herself. So did some of the others.

"You are free to go," Denai said quietly. Gone was all sign of her anger.

Blade thought about it. He glanced at her slim frame huddled forlornly against the wind. At last he said, "You did save my life, Denai. And so I will make you a trade: my life for yours. I will stay with you and your people until the short-faced bear returns for you. I will kill it and save your life. Then we will be even."

"And then you will leave?" she asked.

"*Eeyak.*"

Pensive, she answered in a small voice, "Agreed."

"We are agreed then." He smiled to himself, suddenly feeling better. "Shall we go and see what your brothers are cooking for the evening meal?"

Denai walked beside Blade, unable to believe what had happened. First she had learned that the shaman was responsible for scaring the Willow People—the men in particular—away from her. Second, she now had a husband. A husband! He had agreed to stay with her, and her people, until he killed the bear.

She bit her lip. She felt a kind of numbness about the first revelation. The bear. Wild Dog had predicted it would kill her and her mate. How did Wild Dog know such things? she wondered. She feared him. Feared his power.

And what about Blade? Blade would then save her life as she had done for him. It was a fair trade, she decided at last. And one that she could accept.

She smiled up at him. He was brave, braver than the Willow men. He was willing to fight the short-faced bear for her.

He met her eyes, his unsmiling. Once she had believed she would never have a husband. Yet now she did. A tiny flicker of joy unfurled in her heart. Would she ever have children? Ah, no, she must not think such things. It was enough that she had a husband, even if only for a short time.

Uneasily she remembered Chert. He had been willing to fight the bear to protect her. And he had died.

Would the bargain she had just made with Blade mean death for him, too?

Chapter Eight

Two days later, Denai, Blade and her three brothers returned to the camp of the Willow People. Everyone had moved and the new camp was set up beside a small creek. Denai was not surprised that her people had moved; they moved every few days. The domes of the brush huts of their old camp could still be seen some distance away.

Three camp dogs stalked stiff-legged up to the newcomers and snarled. Two of them sniffed at Dirk and Trout, recognized their familiar scent and stopped snarling. The third, however, a huge half-wolf, continued to growl. When the dog sniffed Blade, its lips drew back to expose sharp white teeth. Denai spoke to the dog. "Stop, Sentry! This is a friend!" The dog's growling continued. Blade stood his ground.

"Sentry!" ordered Flint. The dog gave one last snarl at Blade, then trotted away.

A little girl of about six summers ran up to Denai. "Where were you?" the child cried. "I was looking for you!"

Denai smiled and dropped to her knees to hug the girl. "I went to another camp for a time, Grasshopper," she answered gently.

"I want to play with you!" Grasshopper announced. Thereupon, she attached herself to Denai's leg and would not let go, so Denai hobbled along with the child clinging to her. After several steps, Grasshopper tired of the play and ran off with two other children.

Denai sighed. How she wanted a child just like Grasshopper. *Stop it*, she ordered herself. *Grasshopper is here; enjoy your time with her. Do not ask for more.*

Blade watched her, his face impassive.

Flint asked, "Is there anything back at the old camp that you wish to get, Denai?"

"*Eeyak*, there are some baskets and herbs in my hut," she answered. Then shyly, "Some gifts from the marriage festivities, also."

Flint considered. "Someone should go back with you, then, to help you carry and to keep watch against lions." He glanced around. "Dirk? Trout?"

"I will help her," said Blade, stepping forward.

Denai and Flint gaped at him. Flint frowned, considering. Denai knew the problem her brother pondered: would she be safe alone with her new mate?

The past few days traveling with her brothers and Blade had actually been rather pleasant for Denai. Though Blade had acted angry ever since his capture, his anger seemed to be diminishing. She wondered if the bargain they had made helped him to accept being with her people. She had not told her brothers of the bargain she and Blade had made. Nor would she.

"Do let him come with me," she said quickly, before Flint could deny the request. She glanced at Blade. Could she trust him? Was she safe with him? Would he try to hurt her, or would he escape at the first opportunity?

She narrowed her eyes, gauging the distance from the new camp to the old one. Less than half a day's travel there and back, she judged. And she would be in sight of her people. If Blade was going to run, he could do it with ease once they left the Willow camp. Denai would be safe because she could easily find her people, unless he chose to hurt her or kill her before he escaped. She eyed him assessingly.

His dark eyes were veiled as he watched her.

He must know something of my problem, she thought. *Can I trust you?* she wanted to ask.

She made a decision. He would go with her. It would be a test for him, and for herself. "Let him come," she repeated.

Flint eyed the two of them. "Very well," he said at last. "It is not far. You can be back by evening." It was a command. He stared at Blade.

Blade nodded. Flint appeared satisfied. He gave a little nod to Trout, then turned to Denai. "Take Sentry with you."

Denai, Blade and the big dog set off, heading for the old Willow camp.

As they walked along, just the two of them, Denai wondered what to say. Blade did not seem bothered by the uncomfortable silence between them. She wondered if Sentry's constant warning growls alarmed him. If they did, he did not show it.

The gravel under her sandaled feet crunched as she walked along. Birds twittered and flitted among the

105

low sage and rabbitbrush plants. The wind blew across the dry landscape. And still he did not speak.

They reached the brush huts. Denai ducked into her hut, leaving Blade and Sentry waiting outside. Sentry growled low in his throat. Would Blade escape while she picked up her baskets and herbs? If he was going to escape, now would be the time, she mused.

She had received two baskets as wedding gifts and she carefully packed away her stone knives, scrapers and awls in them. Finally, she was ready. She ducked back out of the hut, expecting him to be gone.

He watched the horizon, back the way they had come. When he turned to face her, his dark eyes were unreadable.

"I am ready," she said, lifting all three of her baskets. They started walking back to the new camp, Sentry running ahead. The sun beat down on their heads. She was hot from walking, but there was no shade anywhere. There was an occasional bush, but mostly the land was treeless here. She plodded on. "Why do you not say something?" she demanded irritably after a while.

He shrugged. "I have nothing to say."

She grimaced and walked a little faster.

Blade let her walk ahead, amused at her obvious frustration with him. He glanced around, as he always did, keeping watch for lions or saber-tooths or any other predators as they walked along. But there were no animals that he could spy. The dog, mean tempered as he was, would alert them to any lions or wolves.

Blade ambled along. So her brothers had agreed to let him accompany her, had they? He'd surprised even himself by saying he would go with her. Now why had he done that? he wondered. To escape? *Dak*, he mused. He could have done that easily once he was with her. Though he was tempted, he had not escaped. He had stayed.

But then, he had made that bargain with her. It was interesting that she had agreed to have him stay to kill the bear. After all, she had three brothers, and any one of them would be a match for a bear, in his opinion. She wanted him to kill it.

But once their bargain was complete, Blade would leave. That was certain.

He wondered where the bear lived, what it looked like. He must get a description from her. The sooner he killed it, the sooner he could go on his way.

He glanced at Denai. She strode along, ignoring the streams of sweat pouring off her. Clearly she wanted to get back to the Willow camp as quickly as possible.

Perhaps his silence on this walk would bank the flames of hope he saw in her big dark eyes. Hope that he and she would have something like a true marriage.

He snorted aloud. The dog, Sentry, glanced at him, yellow eyes burning, and gave a low snarl. Blade ignored him.

A true marriage was not something Blade wanted. Not at all. He did not want a woman. And he did not want Denai, even if she was strong. Even if her eyes were big and dark and a man could get lost in them. And even if her breasts were a pleasant sight. She was not for him. No woman was.

He surveyed the sandy hills. No animals stalking them. Good. His grip on his spear tightened. They would be back with her people soon.

He glanced at the ground again. There were the

footprints he and Denai had made on the way to the old camp. The dog's, too. But now there was a third set of human tracks. Someone had been following them. Who?

He glanced back at the old camp and thought he saw someone duck behind a hut. *Eeyak*, they were being followed.

He pursed his lips thoughtfully and regarded Sentry. The dog ran along, sniffing the tracks. He wagged his tail and headed for the old camp.

"Sentry, come!" Denai ordered sternly. The dog trotted over to her. It was someone the animal knew then. . . .

Blade said to Denai, "Let us walk faster. After all, we must reach camp by nightfall. Flint said so."

Her only answer was a rude glower.

It had been a mistake to accompany her, he thought now. He had to watch her walk, her movements graceful. He had to wonder about her, what she was thinking, what she was feeling, if she liked him. *Stop it*, he ordered himself. *Denai of the Willow People is not the woman for me.*

He could ignore her slim body, her scent, he told himself.

Once, he turned around quickly and discerned a man who flattened himself to the ground behind a thick bush. Blade smiled grimly to himself. Now, who was that following them? Who, indeed.

It was dusk when they finally walked into the Willow camp. Blade pretended not to notice the watchful stares of two of Denai's brothers, nor the curious looks that Rabbit Woman and Pika gave him. But he knew they watched him, that they wondered if he had treated Denai well. It appeared that Trout was missing, he noted sardonically.

Once in camp, Sentry trotted over to Flint's hearth.

Denai hurried ahead and followed the dog over to her brother's fireside. Blade waited at a little distance as she spoke with Flint and Dirk. They eyed him warily, but whatever she told them must have been positive, because he saw Flint laugh, and Dirk relaxed his tense stance. Denai looked amused when she left her brothers, and he wished he knew what she had said.

She walked over to him. "It is time to eat and then we will rest," she said.

They joined her brothers beside the fire. Flint gestured hospitably for Blade to sit down. Denai sat a little distance away from him, but he could feel her eyes upon him.

Suddenly Trout emerged from the gathering evening gloom. Dirk handed Blade and Trout each a stick with a steaming chunk of roasted meat on it. Blade took a bite. For the first time he felt awkward. He was eating his enemies' meat.

The next day, with Sentry at her side, Denai helped Blade gather branches and brush. They dragged them to a spot not far from her brothers' huts. Together Blade and Denai built a brush hut.

The dog dozed in the shade of the branches and lifted his head to snarl at Blade now and then.

Silence reigned between Blade and Denai. When Denai's hut was completed, they wove the branches together for a hut for Blade, again working in silence. Unaccountably, Blade found himself growing annoyed that she did not speak to him.

And he ruthlessly quashed any feelings of pleasure

at her companionship. They were working together, that was all. He was with her for a short time. After the short-faced bear was killed he would leave her, he reminded himself sharply.

When the huts were finished, she surprised him. She went to one of her brothers' huts and returned with a spear. "I am going hunting," she announced. "You may come with me or not, as you wish."

He raised a brow. "The women of the Willow People hunt?" he asked.

"I do," she answered.

He eyed her. "It is unusual for a woman to hunt, is it not?" Among his own people, the Lion People, women did not hunt, but he would not tell her that because then he would have to tell her all about his people. And he refused to do that.

"I am the only Willow woman who hunts," she admitted. When she met his eyes, her dark ones were bright with unshed tears. "When my brothers and I finally understood that no Willow man was going to marry me, my brother Trout taught me to hunt. My brothers did not want me to go hungry while they were gone hunting for a long time." She paused, then went on. "None of the Willow People complained, certainly not the men."

He glanced away from the pain he saw on her face. It had obviously hurt her that none of the Willow men had wanted her. "I do not complain," he replied brusquely.

"Then let us go," she said. "We will not take Sentry. He will scare the game."

Blade said, "Flint will want to know where we go."

"Flint?" She glanced around. "Oh. *Eeyak*, I had better tell him."

Blade eyed her. "And be sure to invite Trout. Otherwise, while we stalk deer, he will be stalking us."

"What do you mean?" she asked.

"Trout followed us yesterday." Blade lifted one shoulder in a shrug. "I thought you knew." Then he grimaced. "Your brothers do not trust me."

"Should they?" she asked pertly.

"No," he answered.

"I did not see Trout's tracks," she mused. "But you did."

Blade could not tamp down a twinge of satisfaction when he saw admiration in her dark eyes.

They smiled at each other.

Chapter Nine

Late one afternoon, Denai, Blade and Trout walked into the Willow camp. A deer was slung over Blade's shoulders. It was Denai's kill. She had skinned it and gutted it herself. She glanced proudly at the carcass and assured herself she was looking at the deer, not the man.

Flint greeted them, Sentry trotting at his heels. The big dog growled when he saw Blade.

Flint patted the dog's gray head approvingly. "Uncle Rhino has called a meeting. He wants you to join in."

Denai and Trout ambled over to where the rest of the Willow People had gathered. Blade followed slowly.

Once all the Willow People had assembled, the short decision-maker began, "It is time for our people to move again. I have been thinking about this for some time. I think it would be good for us to travel to the mammoth water hole."

Denai remembered the place. It was a marsh, a shallow lake grown thick with water plants around the rim. She smiled to herself, glad her people were going to go there.

There were several grunts of approval at Uncle Rhino's words.

"That is a good place to hunt," Flint said.

"Many birds live there," a woman volunteered.

"Mammoths drink there," Dirk observed.

"And lions," Pika added with a giggle. She slid a coy glance at Dirk and giggled again.

"I like the tasty wapato plants that grow there," said Rabbit Woman.

"Many animals drink the refreshing water at mammoth water hole," Uncle Rhino continued. "It will be good hunting for our men."

"Short-faced bears," said Wild Dog, the shaman, "will come to drink there, too."

No one spoke. Eyes downcast, Denai clenched her fists at her sides. When she finally looked up, she saw that the Willow People watched her curiously. She grimaced.

"It is decided, then," Uncle Rhino said forcefully. "We will leave for the marsh. Tomorrow."

With nods of agreement, the Willow People dispersed back to their huts.

"Do you like to hunt mammoths?" Denai asked as she and Blade walked over to her brothers' fire.

Blade slid the deer carcass off his shoulder. "Sometimes."

"I remember how intently you watched the mammoth herd that day on the hill," she said. "You seemed so interested in them. I wondered then if you wanted to hunt them."

"Any man welcomes the chance to hunt mammoths."

She had to agree with that. Her brothers greatly enjoyed a mammoth hunt. Mammoths, because of their size, aggressive temperament and numbers, were one of the most dangerous animals to hunt, but her brothers relished the challenge.

Trout came up behind them and clapped a friendly hand on Blade's back. "Perhaps you will hunt mammoths with us when we reach the mammoth water hole."

Blade's handsome face registered surprise at Trout's suggestion. Denai frowned. Her brothers wanted this man to hunt with them?

"We can always use another man with a good eye and a strong spear in our hunting group," Trout continued, his hand sliding off Blade's shoulder. "Have you hunted mammoths before?"

"A time or two," Blade answered stiffly. Denai thought he did not seem to like Trout's friendliness. She did not like it either, though she was baffled as to why.

"Denai said that you saw my tracks when I followed you to the old camp," Trout said jovially.

Blade's mouth twisted. "Your tracks were obvious. So were the three times you lay down on the ground to hide yourself from my view."

Trout chuckled. "Four times," he corrected. "We could use a man with good tracking skills."

Was it jealousy she was feeling? pondered Denai.

Was she jealous that her brothers wanted to include Blade?

"Now that you are one of our people, you may want to join a hunting group. You could hunt with my brothers and me."

"I will think on it," Blade answered in a distant voice. Trout nodded and wandered away.

"You do not seem pleased with Trout's offer," Denai observed.

Blade shrugged. He crossed his arms over his chest and stared down at her. "You and I both know that I will only stay until I have killed the short-faced bear."

Denai glanced down at the fire, unable to hold his calm, unreadable black eyes. How had she so swiftly forgotten that he would leave once the bear was killed?

They spoke no more about him joining her brothers' hunting group. Denai took out her knife and sliced meat off the deer carcass. "I will prepare the evening meal," she announced.

He grunted and sat down beside the brush hut they had built for him. He took up his spearhead and began chipping the edges, making the sharp blade even sharper.

She sprinkled a handful of herbs on the deer meat, then slid the meat onto clean sticks and roasted the chunks over the fire. The smell of the sizzling meat caused Blade to glance up, his nose lifted into the air.

She smiled and picked up one of the sticks. She carried it over to him and, using a leaf, pulled the meat off the stick and handed it to him. "For you," she said.

Frowning, he took the meat and tasted it. He did not thank her or make any comment, merely chewed. She turned away, disappointed.

115

When her brothers gathered at the fire, she gave them their meat in the same way. They joked and talked among themselves, while she quietly ate her piece of roasted meat. Though she had used aromatic herbs, the meat tasted like dirt in her mouth. Dirk offered a second meat stick to Blade, but he refused.

He does not like the food I prepare, she thought in despair. How could she be a good wife to him if he did not like her cooking? Her appetite gone, she poked at the fire listlessly with an empty meat stick. Drippings of fat on the end made the flames sputter and then flare up. She supposed he preferred the food his first wife had prepared.

Blade watched Denai as she poked at the fire, prodding the embers. The food she had prepared tasted delicious—so delicious his mouth still watered for another piece of meat sprinkled with herbs. But he had forbidden himself a second piece, and called upon his formidable Lion's training to do so. He would not depend on her in any way, he warned himself. He would not enjoy the food she prepared. When Dirk offered him some meat, he turned away as though it cost him no effort. He was proud of his refusal.

He heard the brothers talking and did not join in. Once or twice he detected his name in the conversation, but he gave no sign that he knew they spoke of him. It was obvious they wanted him to join their hunting group. First Trout, then Flint had asked him to join. He had to make a decision soon. They would wonder why he did not join his wife's brothers to hunt. Indeed, all the Willow People would wonder why.

His gaze moved beyond the brothers to where their sister sat. His wife.

Dak. He would not think of her as such. She did not

look like his wife, Amethyst. His wife had had huge brown eyes like a fawn, not leaf-shaped eyes. His wife had had long black hair, loose, unadorned, not tied back at the nape. His wife had had a sturdy, strong frame, with voluptuous breasts, not a long, lithe body like an antelope. No, this was not his true wife.

Blade covered his eyes. Why did he still waste time thinking about Amethyst? He could have saved her if he had stayed with her. *Dak*, he did not want a wife again. Ever.

He glanced up to see Trout watching him. Great Mother, could he never get away from their watchful gazes? Could he endure until his bargain was complete or would he be driven to escape before then by frustration?

Blade rose and strode from the fireside, anxious to put space between himself and the Willow men. He took several deep, calming breaths of evening air. He must think upon what to do.

He studied the stars over his head. As long as he was with the Willow People, they would be suspicious of him. He was a stranger to them, unknown, and they did not trust him. Yet the brothers expected, even wanted, him to stay and be a husband to their sister. What to do? he pondered.

It would be so easy to escape, he thought. *Let her brothers kill the bear when it returns.*

He could lull the brothers' suspicions and then, when they were not so vigilant, he could escape. He would be far away from their camp by the time the brothers started to track him. He had excellent tracking and hunting skills himself, equal to theirs or better, he judged.

He stared at the stars, pondering. The bright light

117

of the full moon made it difficult to see some of the stars he knew. He sighed. And what if he did escape? Then he would be free again, free to wander the hills alone. Strangely, the thought of freedom did not fill him with the elation it had when he was first captured.

Well, he would worry about that later, he decided. For now it was best to fool the brothers into thinking that he had accepted his lot with them, that he had no plans to escape.

What about your bargain with Denai? asked a little voice in his mind. *You said you would stay and kill the bear.*

Need I honor a bargain made with the enemy? he wondered. *That is all it is. I cannot be held to it. She cannot hold me to it; she is only a weak woman.*

He tamped down the gnawing of his conscience. Denai had her brothers. Let them look after her.

Her brothers. *Eeyak . . .* her brothers. What was he going to do about her brothers?

He glanced at them. Flint quickly started chipping at a spear point he was making. Dirk frowned and jiggled a stick in the fire, staring intently at it as though he were fire-hardening the stick. Trout closed his eyes and his face took on an impassive look, as though he had been sleeping. Blade snorted to himself. Strange how all three brothers had suddenly found something to do. But he knew better. They had been watching him.

He would have to lull their suspicions, he decided. And what better way to do it than to pretend to be kind to their sister?

As Blade returned to the fire, Sentry growled low in his throat. That dog needed to be lulled, too, thought Blade with a grimace as he stepped away from the animal. "Lie down," Flint commanded, and the big brute slunk over to lie next to the fire.

Blade sidled over to where Denai sat weaving a basket by firelight. He reached out a hand to her. She looked up at him as if she did not understand his unspoken invitation.

"Come and walk with me," he said in a low, calm voice. Feigning kindness, he gently helped her to her feet. He almost laughed aloud at how wide her eyes grew. She wanted to believe that he liked her, that he wanted to walk with her. He slid a glance toward her brothers. They, too, were staring, Flint and Dirk open-mouthed.

The only one not fooled by his deceptive gestures was the dog, Sentry. The huge dog snarled, lifting his lips to show sharp canines. He half rose. "Down," Flint commanded. Still snarling, the huge beast lowered his belly to the ground again.

Eeyak, Blade must come up with a plan for Sentry, too.

Blade took Denai's hand and led her away from the fire. He could hear movement behind him. Trout had left his place at the fire to follow them.

Blade walked along, speaking calmly to Denai, pointing out certain stars to her and telling her the names he called them by. She said nothing, but her huge eyes followed every move he made.

Her hand was warm in his grip and her fingers tightened imperceptibly now and then on his. Trout still followed them, though the noise he made grew fainter, as if he were allowing them a greater distance for privacy.

What fools her brothers are, Blade thought, *if this is all it takes to deceive them . . . a walk in the moon-*

light, holding Denai's hand, talking in a gentle voice to her. . . .

He touched her upturned face as she gazed at the stars. "You are very beautiful," he murmured.

She gasped and he wondered if Trout heard it. He smiled to himself and ran his finger across her cheekbone. "Very beautiful." He leaned toward her.

He lowered his lips to hers. He could feel her warm breath on his mouth. Just as he would have kissed her, the heavy weight of an angry dog slammed against his legs. Flung off balance, Blade flailed out his arms and caught Denai's shoulders, breaking his fall. He could feel her brace herself as she steadied him. Quickly, not wanting her support, he dropped his hands and whirled to face the snarling dog.

"Sentry!" Trout cried, panting. He tore the dog away. "Come with me," he ordered the dog, yanking the animal back.

Man and growling dog withdrew, back to the fire.

Denai asked in a small voice, "Did he bite you? Are you hurt?"

Blade grimaced. It would take more than a snarling dog to hurt him. *"Dak,"* he answered sullenly, angry that his audience was gone and his pretense destroyed by the dog. "Let us return to camp." It was not worth his effort if her brothers were not there to see.

They returned to the camp in silence. He slanted a glance at Denai. She looked ready to cry, as if she had been sorely disappointed. Well, so had he. His plan to fool her brothers had been interrupted. That was what was frustrating him. *Eeyak,* that was it.

Chapter Ten

Denai trudged along, carrying her heavy baskets. She stopped once, set down her baskets and wiped the sweat from her eyes with her arm. Oh, it was so hot, walking across the hills in the bright sun! Her people had rested at midday, avoiding the hottest part of the day, but it helped little.

In front of her and behind her snaked the line of Willow People. Her eyes sought out Blade's tall form. She spotted him talking with Trout. Jealousy arose within her. He was her husband; he should be talking with her!

Just as quickly, she swallowed her feelings. He had been forced to marry her, she reminded herself. He was not a true husband. He would stay only until he killed the short-faced bear, Evil One.

But at least she had that much, she thought as she watched Blade stride along. Every now and then he halted and scanned the landscape. He watched for predators that might sneak up on the Willow People as they traveled. She felt happy inside, knowing he was protecting her.

He glanced her way and she gave a tiny wave. He answered with a slight nod, then turned away to talk to Trout again.

She grimaced. He would rather talk to her brother than to her. How well she knew that. He was careful never to be alone with her.

As she watched him, he left Trout and came toward her. He walked proudly, his broad shoulders back, his black hair fluttering in the wind. Each step he took was confident. Her heart slammed in her chest. What should she say to him? He was coming to talk with her; she knew it.

And then he was standing in front of her. He gazed down at her, his dark eyes allowing her to see only that distant, infuriating calm of his, a kind of shield he wore that sheltered the true man and his thoughts from her as effectively as yellow paint shielded a shaman. She dropped her gaze, her mind searching frantically for something to say.

"I will walk with you for a time," he said. His deep voice sent shivers down her spine.

She nodded, not trusting herself to say anything. He strode effortlessly at her side. She was panting to keep up with his steps. The baskets she carried were heavy, while he carried only his spear and a few bags tied at his waist. Still, she hurried along, not wanting him to leave her behind. He must have seen what a struggle it was for her to keep up, because he slowed his pace.

"Have you been to the mammoth water hole before?" he asked.

She nodded. "Two summers ago we visited it." She cringed inside at how squeaky her voice sounded. Truly, she must be the mouse that Rabbit Woman accused her of being.

"I will carry that basket for you," he said, and she wanted to melt into the gravel at his feet at the kindness she heard in his voice. She could not meet his eyes as she passed him a basket, the heaviest one, the one that held the meat and a deer robe she used as a blanket on cold nights.

He accepted the basket and they walked in silence for a time. She wondered if the other men would tease him for carrying a basket—women's work, in the Willow People's estimation.

Luckily none of the Willow men said anything as they continued to walk along, though she thought she saw approval in Trout's dark gaze when he glanced in their direction. She blushed and concentrated on putting one foot in front of the other. She hoped they would reach the water hole soon. Then she remembered that Uncle Rhino had said several days must pass before they reached the marsh.

When the Willow People stopped for a rest, Denai and Blade shared dried meat and roots. Denai was surprised that Blade stayed nearby; he even sat close to her. And when Dirk gestured to Blade to come over and sit and talk with her brothers, Blade refused. "I will stay with Denai," he answered casually.

Denai's whole body warmed at his words. He wanted to spend time with her! She caught Flint's small nod of approval to Dirk.

Rabbit Woman watched them, a surprised expression on her face. Denai could not resist a smug smile in Rabbit Woman's direction. *I do not have to hunt*

123

this man down like a lioness the way you hunt Trout,
she would have said if she had dared to say anything.
But Denai stayed where she was. Blade was sitting
close to her and that was all that mattered for now.

When Uncle Rhino gave the word, everyone got to
his or her feet and began walking once again. The day
passed slowly, with Blade solicitously carrying the
basket most of the time. Now and then he would hand
it back to her and leave with the men to see what was
over the next hill, but then soon he would come loping
back to her. Denai tried to keep her heart from pounding at each reappearance, but she was unsuccessful.

During the next rest, Denai had to restrain herself
from staring at Blade's handsome profile. Her gaze fell
to his hands. He was repairing an obsidian spear tip.
She watched his hands, which were large and clean,
the fingers tapered. As did all the other men, Blade
spent much of his time working with and repairing
the stone-tipped spears he carried. Lives depended on
the state of the weapons.

Thoughtfully, Denai rose to her feet and went to
speak to Flint. She returned with what she hoped
would be a welcome gift for Blade: a piece of fine-
grained gray chert with a red stripe running through
it. When she had asked Flint for the chert, he had not
questioned her as to why she wanted the good-quality
stone; he had merely handed it to her, stating that the
chert would make a strong spear point. Perhaps he
guessed what she was going to do with the stone,
mused Denai.

Shyly Denai walked over to where Blade sat chipping at the black obsidian. She squatted down beside
him, reluctant to interrupt him. She waited until he
stopped chipping. Then quietly, fearing her words

would be drowned out by the pounding of her heart, she said, "I would like to give you this." She held out the fist-sized piece of chert.

Blade glanced at it. He hesitated, and she saw his jaw clench. He returned to his work. "I have enough stone," he said gruffly.

He had refused her gift! "Aaaiiee," Denai cried in mortification. She dropped the chert and fled. She did not go near Blade for the rest of the day. Once she saw him approach Flint and hand the chert back, so she avoided Flint, too, for the rest of the day, lest he see the hurt in her eyes and she see the pity in his.

The remainder of the day passed slowly as Denai trudged across the hot gravel; the sagebrush scratched her legs, and she wished she had never met such a man as Blade.

Later, after choking down the evening meal of rabbit, she sat in the deepening dusk, hiding behind her brothers, and careful to keep her distance from Blade, who sat and laughed with them at their camp fire. She stared at the dancing flames, wondering when she would gain the courage to even look at Blade again.

The memory of him returning her gift still made her want to curl up in a little ball and hide. How had she so misread his kindnesses to her?

Suddenly noticing that the only sound she heard was the crackle of the fire, Denai glanced up. Her brothers had discreetly withdrawn to visit other people in the Willow camp. They had left her alone with Blade.

Mortification flooded over her anew and she wanted to leap to her feet, but unfortunately her legs did not obey her. So she sat there, lumplike, her cheeks growing hot with embarrassment.

"Do not hide in the dark, Denai," Blade said.

"I am not hiding," she said with as much dignity as she could drag up from inside herself. She edged a little closer to the fire. She would not be the mouse that Rabbit Woman named her.

"Do you go hunting with my brothers?" she asked boldly, telling herself that she would not let his rejection of her gift bother her. *Dak,* she would not.

He glanced at her, and she saw his eyes flash. Then the emotion was hidden, replaced by that dark veil in his eyes that hid his thoughts so well. "*Eeyak.*"

She should be glad he was going to hunt with her brothers, she told herself. He was acting as her husband in front of the Willow People. Yet there was a tiny twinge of disappointment, too, that he would choose to leave her to go with them. Then she remembered her gift of chert and his refusal. She squeezed her eyes shut. It was best if she did not want too much from this man, she warned herself.

Blade had his head back and was staring up at the sky. She followed his gaze to the stars and remembered how he had walked with her that night, naming the stars in his deep voice. She'd thought then that perhaps there was hope that they would have—No! she warned herself. Better not to hope for a true marriage with him . . .

"The other night," she said softly, "you told me about the stars and their names. Tonight I will tell you a story, a story that my Willow People tell."

He glanced at her. She could not tell if he was interested in what she said or not, but she decided she would pretend he was and try, one more time, to touch him.

"Long, long ago," Denai began, sliding a quick

glance at him, "there was only the Great Mother. She had made the vast lands, the plains, the hills, the sagebrush, the pine trees, the water, and all the animals, birds and insects. The stars, too."

Blade was watching her. She had to pretend that he was not, or her voice would surely tremble. "The Great Mother looked over all that She had made and found it to be very good. So every day She would rise from her sleeping mats when the sun rose and She would watch the animals hunt and play. She would watch the tiny ant build its home. She would listen to the pine trees sigh in the wind, and hear the hummingbird sing its song with its wings.

"But one morning Great Mother did not rise from Her mats with the sun. She stayed on Her mats and lay there, unhappy. Something was missing. Great Mother was lonely. It was not enough for Her to watch the animals play and the grasses grow and the birds sing. The next day it was the same. Great Mother would not get out of Her bed. This went on for many, many days.

"Then one bright morning, Great Mother started to cry in Her loneliness. As She cried, a tear rolled down one cheek. The tear splashed onto the floor of Her hut and turned into a little girl. A second tear rolled down Her cheek and turned into a little boy. Then a third tear, and a fourth tear. All, all turned into a little girl or boy. Soon, Great Mother's hut was filled with the laughing, happy voices of children.

"Then Great Mother smiled. While the children played and sang and ran and jumped, Great Mother pounded many roots together, then mixed the powder with water in a pot. She cooked and cooked the mixture until it became a thick gruel. When the gruel was

127

done, She sprinkled honeydew, the sweet droppings from the insect, onto the gruel. Then She fed the gruel to the children.

"The children ate the gruel, and as they ate, they grew and grew and turned into adults. Soon there were so many adults in Her hut that Great Mother's hut was ready to burst open. Then She kissed each adult on the forehead, to give them wisdom, and sent them out into the world. Though they forgot their time with Great Mother, they had Her kiss of wisdom to help them through many trials.

"And so each adult met a mate and married and made families of their own. And that is how our Willow People came to be on the Earth," Denai finished softly.

Was Blade asleep? She could not tell, he was so still and quiet.

But telling the story had relaxed Denai, and she felt kindly toward him. Half hoping he was truly asleep, she took courage and added, "I sometimes wonder where the Great Mother is now, and if She's watching Her people. Or if She has forgotten them. And me. Sometimes I think She has forgotten me." Denai leaned a little closer to Blade. "I tell you true, I think the Great Mother does not like me. Else why would She have let the bear take away the good man I was to marry?"

Blade rose to his feet. By the fire, she could see that his lips were tight, his face cold and hard. What had she said?

He stalked away, leaving her sitting by the fire. Denai put her head in her hands. Tears squeezed between her fingers. She had tried. She had tried to be kind to Blade, tried to share some part of herself with him so that he would want to be married to her. But no more. No more. She would share nothing with him ever again.

Chapter Eleven

Denai marched ahead of Blade. Today her hair was different—her black hair fanned out behind her, and little braids interwoven in the back of her hair bounced. Her spine was straight and her step firm. Blade caught up with her and sidled along beside her. When he tried to catch her eye, she pointedly looked away. He knew she was doing it on purpose to avoid him. A grim smile curved his mouth.

Let her avoid me, he thought as he moved away to guard the line of people. *That is fine with me. What do I care? I do not want a woman. I do not want a friendship with any of these Willow People. Feelings for them would only hold me back.* And if Denai was not speaking to him it would be that much easier for him to leave her and her people when the time came.

Blade walked along, carrying his spear and constantly surveying the landscape for wolves and lions as part of his duty on the trek. So far he'd seen only one old lion that had tracked them for a time before finally giving up and ambling off.

Sentry, the dog, loped past Blade. "Sentry," called Blade in a low voice. "Come here, dog." But the wolf-like animal growled warningly and trotted on. *I am out of favor with Willow woman and Willow dog,* thought Blade in irritation.

Shrugging, he glanced around the landscape. Far to the south of where they walked was a huge reddish-brown rock butte rearing up out of the sand-colored gravel. It was the only landmark of any interest on the whole horizon, and he wondered curiously if the Willow People would eventually pass by it on their trek to the marsh.

That Denai was not speaking to him irritated Blade further. Last night he had listened, fascinated, to her story about the Great Mother. But when she had told him she thought the Great Mother did not like her because something bad had happened to someone she cared about, it had reminded him too much of what had happened to him and Amethyst. It still troubled him greatly to think upon it.

If Denai but knew the truth, he thought, *she would know that I do not believe there is a Great Mother who cares for Her children. Perhaps there is no one at all. Or if there is a Great Mother, She certainly does not care about anyone, least of all me. Does not Amethyst's death prove that I am alone in my life, with no one to call upon for help, least of all a Great Mother?*

The raging wounds of his anger at the Great Mother had been scraped raw by Denai's words.

Later in the evening, the Willow People made camp for the night in a pine forest, near a small stream.

Uncle Rhino had passed the word that they would stay here for a few days to let the children rest. Several women started making huts. The huts were scattered here and there among the pines.

At the brothers' fireside, after a silent meal in which Blade noticed that Denai sat as far away from him as she could, Flint approached Blade. "Do you wish to join my brothers and me on the hunt tomorrow morning?" he asked.

Blade thoughtfully eyed the sturdy hunter in front of him. Perhaps the excuse of hunting with Flint and his brothers would provide the opportunity Blade needed to escape. Since Denai refused to speak to him, he could expect no long farewells from her, he thought with irony. What did it matter? He cared not at all for what Denai or her brothers thought of him, or whether she talked to him or not! Once he had escaped, Denai and her Willow People would matter as little as a deer carcass stripped clean by lions.

Blade shook his head while a plan formed in his mind. First he would feign reluctance. "Hunt tomorrow morning? *Dak*, I think not."

"Uh," grunted Flint, and Blade could hear his disappointment.

Blade slid a glance at Denai. She had overheard them, and he saw the look of dismay on her face, which she quickly tried to hide. He guessed she wanted him to join her brothers' hunting unit. Well, it mattered little to him what she wanted, for now he was determined to escape on the morrow.

Flint was eyeing Blade. "A man needs other hunters," Flint observed. "A man who wants to succeed at hunting will do better if he has other men to help him."

Inwardly Blade agreed. He had been part of a hunting unit when he had lived among the Lion People. He, his father, his best friend Hunter and two of Hunter's cousins had hunted together and done well. But that was long ago, Blade reminded himself with a shrug. Aloud he said, "I will think on it." He smiled to himself. His words would make it more believable when he later announced his change of plans to join them.

"Do not think on it too long," Flint replied, his brown eyes snapping, "or some of our men will say you do not want to hunt. They will say that you want to sit around and sleep all day and let others bring you meat."

Blade clenched his fists. He answered through clenched teeth, "I hunt. Let no one question me on that."

Flint shrugged. "What a man says, whispers. What a man does, shouts."

Blade glared at him. He knew what Flint was trying to do: get him so angry that he would want to prove himself, but he refused to be caught in that snare. Nonetheless, Flint's words stung.

Blade's hands shook with anger. "Then you will just have to wait until you know if I whisper or shout."

Flint snickered. "We will not wait long, my brothers and I. We will know soon." He started to walk away. "The Willow men are already talking," he added with a sly smile. He strode away.

Blade glared after him. Some part of him wanted to rise up to the challenge in Flint's words and prove that he was a good hunter, that he could work with the other men and provide food for his wife and others. *But I must not get caught in his snare,* Blade warned himself. *I must stay with my plan, I leave tomorrow!*

Somewhat reassured by the reminder of his intent to escape, Blade retired to lie beside the fire. The nights were warm and he had no need of a fur to toss over himself. Across the fire from him, he noticed Denai watching him. Behind her lay the dog, Sentry.

"And what do you think?" Blade challenged her. "Do you say I sit around and let others feed me?" Somehow he could not leave knowing she thought so little of him. The realization jarred him.

She met his eyes across the fire. "I, too, will wait and see," she answered. He saw the challenge in her eyes. Then her voice softened. "I want to believe you."

When he said nothing, she added, "They are good men, my brothers. They will not hurt you if you go and hunt with them."

Now she thought he feared her brothers! She thought he expected them to spear him in the back and say they'd thought he was a deer! Blade bolted upright. "Let me tell you one thing," he said as evenly as he could, "I do not fear your brothers."

She looked at him uncertainly. "Then why do you not hunt with them?"

Because I am going to escape, he wanted to yell. Instead he said with a snarl, "I make the decision when to hunt with them. No one else does."

She grimaced. "You sound like a man bent on doing only his own will, even if it hurts others. That is what such an answer tells me."

"Aaargh!" He snarled. Now she thought he was selfish! He lay back down with a thump and turned his back to her. He would not waste his words and speak to her, would not defend himself any longer. Let her—

and her interfering brothers—think whatever they wanted!

"Blade," he heard her whisper.

"What?"

"I do want to believe you."

A twinge of conscience shook him and he could not answer.

"Good night." Her voice was as soft and caressing as duck's down.

"Good night," he finally answered, his voice rough.

Blade finally slept. He awoke when he heard the brothers leave their places by the fire to go on the hunt. They slipped out quietly into the still, dark night.

When the first streaks of dawn lit the eastern sky, Blade rose and gathered all his possessions, his leather bags, including the one with his great-grandfather's chunk of obsidian, and his spear.

"Where do you go, Blade?" Denai's voice came in a whisper.

He took a deep breath, preparing himself for the lie. "I have changed my mind," he replied evenly. "I go to hunt with your brothers."

She sat up and glanced around. "They have already gone." She sounded worried.

"I will find them and join them," he said. Before she could question this, his traveling alone, something her brothers had not allowed before, he added, "Be sure Sentry does not follow me."

She nodded and put a hand on the dog's gray ruff. "Did Flint or Dirk tell you which way they went?"

He shook his head. "I will follow their tracks." That, at least, was the truth.

There was a silence during which he fumbled for something to say. It was the last time he would see her. Surely—he knew she thought of him as a husband—there was something he should say. But no words presented themselves to his lips.

"Farewell," Denai said softly.

He could not read her dark eyes in the dim light, but he heard the regret in her voice. Did she suspect what he planned? *Dak*, she could not, he told himself.

"Farewell, Denai," he said firmly. He strained to see her in the gloom; he could see her sitting, watching him, her body a dark shape, dark hair to one side. This was his last sight of Denai of the Willow People, he told himself. "Remember to hold Sentry."

"I will," she promised.

Then he was striding in the direction her brothers' tracks went, and pushing Denai out of his mind. He followed the men's tracks a short distance; then he struck out on his own. By midmorning he was far away from the Willow camp, and walking through a forest of pine trees.

Blade had not been gone long before Denai missed him. She wished he would hurry back, but if he was hunting with her brothers, they would come back when they had killed game, and not before. And after Flint had been so rude, doubtless Blade felt he had to bring in meat, she thought. She sighed, wishing she had talked to Blade yesterday. Instead she had let her anger come between them. And now he was gone. And she missed him.

She hoped Flint would treat Blade better when he caught up with her brothers. She knew Flint meant well, but he could be so . . . so rude.

If only she had not been so angry at Blade yesterday.

Perhaps they could have talked, laughed, shared a happy dinner.

But she had been angry at him for stalking away after she had spilled her heart to him. Even now, the memory of telling him how she felt abandoned by the Great Mother—something she'd not told another person, ever—even now the thought brought a flush of mortification to her cheeks. She had told Blade, and he had walked away.

That was why she was so angry. And she was angry at herself, too, for she knew her resolve that she would tell him nothing else would not hold. It was all she could do to keep from running after the man whenever he even glanced her way with those dark, veiled eyes.

Denai squeezed her eyes shut tight, fighting off a simple truth: she was worse than Rabbit Woman when it came to chasing after a man.

Chapter Twelve

Blade smiled into the flames of his first camp fire since he had escaped the Willow People. Escape had been so easy. He had little concern that Denai's brothers would find him, because he had been careful to go in the opposite direction from where they hunted.

Over the fire roasted a hare; gutted and spitted on a stick, it dripped sizzling fat. Blade's stomach growled when he smelled the tantalizing aroma. Rabbit—it would taste good eaten in freedom.

He put another pine stick on the fire. Sticks were dry and plentiful here in the pine woods. Even the thin, brown needles were dried out and burned quickly. He would have to be careful with his fire. The forest was very dry.

He grinned happily. Here he sat, alone. No woman to concern himself with. None of her demanding, suspicious brothers. No one. Just himself. The stars winked above his head. The pine trees surrounded him.

He heard a lion scream in the distant darkness. His smile widened. He need not fear. His spear was close at hand: He had fire. He had food. He was free. He need fear no animal.

And he did not need anyone.

He wondered if wandering alone for two years had changed him. Except for his short stay with the Willow People, he had seen no one since he'd left his Lion People. Now it seemed as if he no longer wanted nor sought out his own kind. He was like a lone lion, or a solitary saber-tooth. Not for him a lion's pride or a noisy, fighting family. *Dak.* He was sufficient unto himself. It was best that way. When he had loved Amethyst he had been almost destroyed by that love. Involvement with other people brought only pain.

And when he was with the Willow People, he'd had a chance to see once again what his own kind were like. They were petty, greedy, and willing to manipulate him to get what they wanted. *Dak*, such games were not for him. He liked being alone.

He saw with satisfaction that the hare was cooked. He took the hot meat off the stick, touching it gingerly so he did not burn his fingers. He ate the meat as though he were a starved man—which he was. Starved for his freedom.

After eating, he buried the bones. It would not do to draw predators in the night. With tired satisfaction he lay down by the fire and slept heavily.

In the morning he awoke. He rose, stretched and yawned. Ah, but it was good to be free.

And the Willow brothers probably did not yet realize he was missing. Blade had wandered deep into the pine forest, walking carefully on the soft needles to hide his tracks from any pursuers. He doubted the Willow brothers were pursuing him yet. They were still hunting, and Denai would not know to warn them that he'd gone.

He squinted at the sun. He probably had another day or possibly two before the brothers found out he was missing. By then he'd be far, far away.

Blade chuckled to himself. He had to admit it had been interesting living with the Willow People. Some of their customs were very different from those of his people. And Denai . . . well, Denai was . . . certainly intriguing. But he was not willing to give up his freedom for a woman. That would mean letting her and probably her three brothers order him around for the rest of his life. Great Mother, no!

He kicked dirt over the remains of his camp fire and made certain the fire was completely dead. Then he picked up his leather bags and spear. Time to move on.

Walking deeper into the pine forest, he hummed as he went along. Great Mother, it was good to be free. He had not realized how onerous it was to be a captive. Never again would he allow others to decide his fate.

He walked for some time before he stopped for a midday meal of leftover rabbit meat. He laid down his spear and sat down on a rock to rest. The air was still and heavy. He glanced overhead, searching the sky. Heavy gray clouds loomed. Suddenly a blue flash of lighting lit the sky. A storm. He smiled and lifted his face up, waiting for the raindrops.

No rain came, but there was another flash of lightning.

A small rattling noise sounded at his feet. He glanced down. Too late he realized he should have been watching where he sat instead of gloating over his newfound freedom.

Moving only his eyes, he saw a baby rattlesnake a mere foot's breadth away, its brown coloring blending in with the brown pine needles and dirt around it.

Blade's spear was just out of reach of his right hand.

He winced inwardly; sweat beaded his brow. Baby rattlesnakes were extremely dangerous. Unlike adult rattlesnakes, they could not accurately gauge how much poison to inject into an enemy. Frequently they shot in too much venom and the prey died a swift, agonizing death.

Sweat coated Blade's forehead and ran down the middle of his back as he sat frozen on the rock. The little snake rattled again, claiming his attention. He inched his right hand closer to his spear. Closer . . . closer . . .

The snake lunged and sank its fangs into the calf of his leg. He felt the small prick, the warm poison . . . then the release when the little snake slithered away.

Blade's eyes widened. Bitten! Great Mother! He shuddered as an image of himself, rolling and foaming on the pine-covered dirt, dying in painful agony, taunted his imagination.

Desperately he leaned over and squeezed blood out of the two tiny puncture wounds the snake had made. So tiny. So deadly!

He could feel the poison creeping up his leg and he squeezed harder. He had to get it out, he had to!

Drops of red blood rolled out, and hope surged through him. He had drained the poison!

But why was it getting difficult to see . . . why were

his fingers suddenly so weak . . . his gut cramping . . . his leg burning?

Great Mother, was he dying? He could not be! He had just tasted freedom, just started to live. . . .

The poison slogged through his body, pushed through his blood with every pounding beat of his panicked heart. He was dying here. In the woods. Alone . . .

He sank to the ground, his limbs weak. The sky was getting darker, closing in around him, and the birds' songs were fading. . . . Were they, too, dying?

Denai's image rose in his mind, her dark eyes staring solemnly at him. Then her face changed to Amethyst's and she screamed at him how she had made love to Hunter. Then Denai's dark eyes were back, and it was her face haunting him, teasing him, admiring him, angry with him, calling him.

Perhaps it would have been a good life with her. . . . Better than this. Better than this . . .

Chapter Thirteen

Denai took another stitch, her fine, white bone needle sliding through the hole in the leather. She drew the thin gut thread carefully, making the stitch just the right tightness. After taking several more careful stitches, she picked up her bone awl and drilled one, then several, round holes through the thick leather and along both sides of the seam she was sewing. Then she switched to the needle again, and pushed it through the awl hole.

"This will be a fine pair of leggings," she muttered to herself. "He had better like them!" Perhaps Blade would like her sewing, since he did not like her cooking.

She continued to sew by the flickering fire. Her brothers and Blade should be returning at any time. They had already been gone two days. She hoped they had much meat and that Blade had been fortunate and killed a deer or antelope of his own.

She sighed. She missed Blade. He had only been in her life a short time, but she missed him.

It was quiet in the camp, with small fires in front of the brush huts. The children appeared to have recovered from the rigors of the walk they'd endured. Grasshopper scampered through the camp, chasing her younger brother.

Denai smiled as she watched the girl run. Grasshopper would be very surprised when she saw the little doll that Denai had made for her. Only a few more quills to sew on the doll's dress and the tiny garment would be finished.

Rabbit Woman and Pika were wandering through the camp, a last walk before settling down for the night. Unfortunately they spied Denai sitting by her fire and walked over. Denai's smile faded from her lips.

"What do you want?" she asked Rabbit Woman.

"The dress."

Denai frowned, perplexed.

"The wedding dress I lent to you," prodded Rabbit Woman. "You still have it, do you not?"

Pika giggled.

Denai rose to her feet and entered her brush hut. She returned with the pale garment over her arm. She handed it to Rabbit Woman. "Perhaps the dress would fit better if it did not have quills sticking in the back," she said evenly.

Rabbit Woman's eyebrows rose. "Whatever is she talking about?" she asked Pika.

Pika shrugged and giggled.

Denai stood defiantly with her hands on her hips.

"Those quills hurt me, Rabbit Woman. They took away all my enjoyment of the dress."

Rabbit Woman shrugged coolly. "It was only a little joke. Can you not laugh at it?"

"I did not find it funny," Denai answered.

"I did," Rabbit Woman replied. She glanced at Pika. "Did you?"

Pika nodded vigorously.

"See? Pika thought it was funny, too. You, Denai, have no understanding of what is funny. And no one wants to be with a woman who does not know how to laugh. I suppose that is why your new husband went off hunting at the first opportunity."

Pika giggled. Rabbit Woman looked smug.

Denai clenched her fists. Why did she always feel so powerless around this wretched woman? "Leave my camp fire," she whispered. "Go. Now!"

"We are happy to leave, are we not, Pika?" answered Rabbit Woman sweetly. She pretended to straighten the dress draped over her arm. "When is Trout due back?" she asked as she was turning away.

"He is not coming back," Denai spat. "He is never coming back. Not to you!"

At first Rabbit Woman looked surprised; then her face creased into a grin. "Oh, that is not what he told me. He told me he would be returning within three nights."

"Then why did you ask me?" Denai said with a snarl.

Rabbit Woman smiled. "Because I wanted to visit with you. Speak with you. I wanted to make certain that Trout's little sister was getting along well, left all on her own." Denai winced at the false note of sympathy in Rabbit Woman's voice.

145

Pika giggled.

"I see, however," Rabbit Woman continued, "that you are an ill-tempered young woman. No wonder your husband wants to go hunting so soon. You do not get along with others, do you?" She sighed, a false sound. "I greatly fear you will drive your new husband away with such bitterness. No man wants to live with a woman who is constantly angry and embittered. It makes for such misery in the home." She smiled sweetly. "Do try to change, Denai." Then she and Pika sauntered away.

Denai stood glaring after them. She wanted to kick something, she was so angry. That woman! How dare she come around and bother Denai with such rude words? How dare she?

Angry, Denai kicked dirt over the fire until there was not a single ember showing. Then she retired to her hut.

But she could not sleep. Rabbit Woman's words spun a web of self-doubt around her. Did Blade truly go hunting because he did not want to be with Denai?

Sadly Denai realized she did not know what to do to please him. She had spent the whole day before he left ignoring him. And then he'd left so suddenly, following after her brothers when they'd already gone on the hunt. It had made Denai truly uneasy. She had feared, momentarily, that he was going to leave.

But he would not do that, she assured herself. He had agreed to stay with her and kill the short-faced bear. He was an honorable man. She hoped. He would keep his word.

Her glance fell on the leggings she'd been sewing for him for the winter. He would return, she thought, hugging the leggings to her chest. He would return and she would speak with him—kindly—and laugh with him. He would want to stay with her. Rabbit Woman was wrong, all wrong.

Chapter Fourteen

He was hot; Great Mother, he was hot. Sweat poured off his skin. He heard the loud crackle of the fire. Smelled the smoke. He opened his eyes and looked around. Was he in the camp of the Great Mother? But why did the Great Mother have such a big fire?

He shook his head and sat up, leaning against the rock for support. He blinked and frowned thoughtfully. This could not be the land where the Great Mother dwelled. *Dak*. It looked too much like the pine forest where he had last been. Except for the fire, of course.

He sat up straighter, his eyes widening. *Fire?*

His body throbbed, but he was alive. The small rattlesnake had misjudged the amount of venom it took to bring down a man. Fortunately the snake had used too little venom.

Fire. Blade staggered to his feet, alarmed now. The

fire burned the sides of the pine trees and crept closer. Blade picked up his leather bags and his spear and started limping away from the startling heat.

A gust of wind came up and he saw the flames behind him fan brighter. His legs shook, but with each step he became stronger and the snake's power receded. He was able to run after a short time.

Blade reached a creek and stepped into the rushing water. The touch of the cold water invigorated him. He glanced around. The fire was creeping down the hill toward him, but he was confident now that he could outrun it—as long as there was no wind.

He glanced out onto the hills. There was sagebrush and grass scattered here and there. The fire might burn itself out once it left the forest and reached those hills.

He darted out of the forest and onto a rough gravel slope.

As he ran he remembered the Willow People. Surely this forest fire would endanger them, too. He glanced over his shoulder. He was outdistancing the flames. Good.

He ran for a time, until he realized he was safe from the fire. He stopped and wiped his brow. The Willow People. They did not know about the fire. They did not know the fire was headed their way. It could come upon them in the night, when everyone was asleep. Burning pines would easily light their brush huts. Some of them might die . . . burned to death in their sleep.

Leave them, he told himself. *The Willow men and women will take care of themselves. There is no need for me to return and warn them. . . .*

But if I do not warn them, some of them might be

caught in the flames . . . and die.

Denai. She does not know the fire is coming.

He stopped. *What should I do?* he wondered. *If I leave here and go into the hills, I can evade the fire and stay free. If I go back and warn the Willow People, I return to certain captivity. Great Mother, what should I do?*

He thought of the Willow brothers. They would be spared. They were out hunting in the hills somewhere. Safe. And they would be more watchful. . . .

But Denai would not be spared. He pictured the panic and fear contorting her face when she saw the flames. She would run . . . all the Willow People would run. There would be great confusion and fear. And no time to take anything with them. Denai would try to help that little girl . . . Grasshopper, wasn't it? But children could not run fast. Children could trip and fall in the panic of running from the flames. *Great Mother, what should I do?*

He glanced back at the flames and the great cloud of smoke. Then he stared out at the clear, beckoning blue sky above the hills . . . and freedom.

With a heavy heart, Blade turned his face toward the Willow camp. It was to be Denai, then.

He set off at a strong lope.

Chapter Fifteen

Denai woke because the hairs on the back of her neck were standing up. A primitive part of her knew someone stared at her. Blade.

"Rise," he said quietly. "We must wake the other Willow People and flee."

She blinked. Then she sat up, shocked at his words. "Flee?"

"There is a big fire in the forest. It comes toward the camp. It will arrive soon."

She rose. "My brothers? Are they here?"

He shrugged. "*Dak.*"

"Are they not with you?" Her voice was sharper than she intended.

"I came alone," he replied. "We must warn the others." He took her hand.

She tugged free. "Wait. I must gather my things." Grabbing up her baskets, she stuffed some meat from last night's meal on top of a deer hide. "I am ready."

They stepped out of the brush hut. It was barely dawn, the sky lightening to the east.

Blade pointed. "You go and awaken those families." He pointed in the opposite direction. "I will awaken these."

She nodded and hurried off. She ducked her head into Grasshopper's dwelling. "Awaken," she cried urgently. "A fire comes!"

Bleary-eyed, blinking, Grasshopper's family took only a short time to get ready. Then they, too, were outside and helping others.

By the time she reached the last hut, all the Willow People were gathered around Blade. She ducked her head inside. The hut belonged to the shaman. "Awaken," she cried. "There is a fire. We must flee!"

The shaman got laboriously to his feet and hurried past her, with only a silent glare at her for her trouble. Denai shrugged and went to join the gathered people. She leaned forward to hear what Blade was saying.

"We must leave now. The fire destroys everything in its path. We must leave now!"

Denai sniffed the air. Smoke! Her heart pounded. Keep calm, she advised herself. She forced herself to focus on Blade. How proud she was of him at this time. He was a true leader, advising her people. But her brothers? Where were they? Had they told Blade to come and warn everyone? She must find out.

Uncle Rhino stepped up to Blade. "Let us leave now," said Uncle Rhino, throwing the weight of his authority behind Blade.

The Willow People set off at a pace fast enough to escape the fire. Men and women carried children so they would not be left behind. Two men passed Denai.

152

They carried an old man between them.

Uncle Rhino walked in the lead, picking the trail by weaving among the pine trees, stopping now and then to hold a pine branch aside to help a young mother or an old man. He called out encouragingly to the stragglers.

Blade walked at the rear of the line. Denai, who had started in the middle of the line, stepped to one side and waited for him.

Pride filled her heart as she watched Blade walk toward her, his stance relaxed. He carried a small boy, Beavertooth, in one arm. Beavertooth was about four summers old.

Her eyes narrowed when she thought she noticed Blade limping and favoring one leg. Then she forgot about it in her admiration of him.

Blade is a brave man, she thought. *My brothers must have recognized this and sent him back to warn us.* Her brow wrinkled. *But where are they?*

As Blade approached she smiled at him. She hoped he had forgotten her surliness the day before he'd left for the hunt. "It is good to see you, my husband," she said quietly.

His eyes widened at that, and for a moment she thought he looked shocked. Then he recovered and nodded. "It is good to see you also, Denai," he answered.

Little Beavertooth made motions that he wanted to get down. Blade set him on his feet and the boy ran to his mother. She scooped him up with a grateful smile at Blade for carrying him.

"My brothers," Denai began, falling into step beside Blade. "Did they send you back to warn us? Are they safe?"

He was quiet for a time, the only sound the padding of their sandals on the soft forest floor. At last he said, "Your brothers are still hunting. I hope they will be able to find us."

He had not answered her question, she realized, but he had brought up a new worry. Would her brothers find the Willow People upon their return from the hunt?

"They know we are heading for the mammoth water hole," she mused aloud. "If they do not find us at the old camp, they will know to go to the marsh." Her reasoning satisfied her; her brothers were not fools. They would find the Willow People. Reassured, she smiled up at him. "I missed you while you were gone," she said. Somehow, after his brave leadership in awakening everyone, and helping them flee the fire in the forest, she felt it was safe to tell him this.

He nodded stiffly, as if he heard her words but did not know what to say. *Do not speak your heart like that,* she reminded herself. *This man shies from my thoughts and feelings like a wounded buck shies from a hunter!*

Her apt comparison brought a sudden bloom of heat to her cheeks as she once more realized how like Rabbit Woman she truly was. Blade was the prey; Denai the hunter. Flustered now, she hid her confusion in silence.

The Willow People marched throughout the day with short stops to rest. Uncle Rhino and Blade held a talk, and it was agreed among the Willow adults that they should walk as far into the night as they could.

But the children started to get tired and the old women and two old men slowed down so much that it was finally decided to call a halt just after sunset.

Exhausted old people and little children would make little headway the next day if they did not rest this night.

The Willow People scattered their possessions around them and sat down. Some of them lay down and were soon snoring. The evening meal was whatever a person had managed to save from the previous night. No camp fires were made.

The smell of smoke from the fire in the forest was weak, and, indeed, the wind had shifted.

"Perhaps we are out of harm's way now," Denai said, handing Blade a piece of meat. "It seems to me that we traveled a great distance this day."

Sitting beside her, Blade took the meat and shook his head. "We must leave the pine forest and walk on the gravel into the hills. Only then will we be safe." His lips tightened as if he had been about to say more but thought better of it.

"What is it?" she asked softly. She met his dark eyes. He looked sad, she thought suddenly.

"The fire," he said at last, reluctantly, "could follow us into the hills. There is grass and sagebrush to feed it. Even in the hills we may not be safe." He glanced around. "But I do not wish to burden your people with words of discouragement."

She nodded. "It will make traveling difficult for them on the morrow," she acknowledged, "if they think they cannot flee the fire."

Their eyes met and Denai felt warm inside as they shared this moment of agreement, small as it was. Hunting with her brothers must have made him feel he was part of her people, she thought shrewdly. He seemed more accepting of her and her people.

She watched him take a bite of the meat. "Did my

brothers kill any antelope? Or deer?" She took a bite of her meat, too.

He chewed slowly, so slowly that she thought he'd forgotten her question. Finally he shrugged his broad shoulders and took another bite of meat. She took his reaction to mean that he did not know if her brothers had found game. Evidently they had found no game while he was with them.

They finished their simple meal and she happened to glance at his leg. There were two streaks of dark, dried blood on the calf and the skin looked puffy. "What happened to your leg?" she asked in surprise.

"Snakebite," he answered.

She squinted at his leg, trying to see it better in the waning light. "I have some herbs I could put on it."

"*Dak*. It is not hurting," he answered gruffly.

"Snakebite is serious," she reproached him. "Some people die from it. Why, when I was a little girl, one of our Willow women died from a snakebite. I still remember it."

"If I was going to die from the bite, I would be dead by now," he replied. "It happened yesterday."

She heard the note of finality in his voice. "I suppose you are correct," she agreed. "I know the snake's poison works quickly." She stared at him, trying to imagine what had happened. She was glad he had not died, glad that he was here with her. But she did not dare tell him that.

"Did my brothers help you when you were bitten?" she ventured finally.

She received no answer. Blade had lain down and turned his back to her. She soon heard rhythmic breathing that told her he was asleep.

With a sigh she lay down and squirmed around on

the ground, trying to find a comfortable position to sleep in.

She rolled onto her back and looked up at the sky. It was clouded over. Perhaps it will rain and put out the fire, was her last thought before she fell asleep.

She awoke the next morning at dawn. Blade was already on his feet, waking people and urging them to rise. Uncle Rhino staggered around trying to get families to waken, too. The shaman was the last one called to get up.

Denai yawned and took little Grasshopper's hand to help the bleary-eyed child walk along. "I hope we reach the hills this day," Denai muttered.

Blade heard her as he walked past. "Even if we do not, I think it will rain and put out the fire." The air was heavy, with a thickness to it. Low gray and white clouds covered the sky.

Raindrops began to fall as they walked. The Willow People were able to seek shelter from the heavy downpour by hiding under rocky ledges.

Hours later Blade glanced at Denai where she crouched beside him under the rock ledge. The tiny space they were squeezed into accurately reflected his feelings. He felt trapped.

He was back with the Willow People, and this time by his own choice. He had wakened them in time to save them from the fire. Did that mean he must live with them forever? he wondered.

"The rain has stopped," Denai observed, holding her hand out from under the rock ledge. "See?" She drew her hand back. It was dry.

Blade crawled out from under the ledge. He stood up, stretching. Bit by bit, other members of the Willow People crawled out from under rocky overhangs. Soon

157

they were gathered in a group around their decision-maker, Uncle Rhino.

"Let us make a fire for the night," he intoned. "The great fire in the forest is dead. No fire could live through this day of rain."

There were grunts of agreement as the people began gathering up dry twigs lodged in the rocks.

Blade got out his fire drill and knife and shaved off some wood for Denai's fire. Then he took his spear and went hunting for a short time. He saw several of the other men slip away and knew they were out snaring or hunting. He returned with two fat hares.

While he was gone Denai must have dug up some roots, for she was just dropping them into the fire to roast as he returned. He saw her profile outlined by the fire. She was not pretty like Amethyst, he thought darkly. Where Amethyst was voluptuous, Denai was slim. Where Amethyst was bright and lively, Denai was quiet. No, she was nothing like what he had known a woman to be, he thought with a sigh.

She glanced up at him and smiled. *Her eyes are soft though,* he told himself, surprised at the truth of it. *And her skin is smooth. She is good to look at,* he thought with a sudden pang.

He glanced away. He did not want to be finding good things about his Willow wife. He had made a bargain with her, a bargain about killing a bear, and it appeared that he was being forced to keep it. "I brought some meat," he said, handing her the two gutted, skinned rabbits.

She took them and spitted them on two long sticks and stuck them next to the flames. When they were cooked, she took one of the rabbits and gave it to Grasshopper's family. Grasshopper's father had returned from the small hunt with nothing.

Blade and Denai had just finished eating their rabbit when Trout, Dirk and Flint walked into camp. "Ho!" cried Trout. "Were you hiding from us?" he joked.

People laughed, and Rabbit Woman's laugh was the loudest of all. "Welcome back," came the happy cries as everyone swarmed around the three brothers.

Flint threw down an antelope, butchered and quartered. "Poor hunting," he said, "but at least it is something."

"It is fine," assured Uncle Rhino. "We will use the meat to replenish our strength from our long walk."

There were nods and happy, excited cries from those who had eaten dried meat or none at all.

Blade continued to sit at his fire, though he gave a slight nod when he saw Flint glance contemptuously in his direction. He wondered how soon it would be before Denai discovered that he had not gone hunting with her brothers.

Not long, as it turned out. She came stomping over to him after having a short talk with Flint and Dirk.

From the fiery flash in her eyes, Blade wondered if he had underestimated her. She surprised him. Perhaps she was as vibrant as Amethyst.

"Where were you?" she said in a hiss, hands on hips. "My brothers say they never saw you while they hunted. They say they thought you were still sitting around camp, eating the meat others worked to provide!"

Blade took a breath. He did not want to lie to her, not after he had chosen to return to the Willow People. On the other hand, how could he tell her he had left her, had escaped, without seeing the passion die in those dark eyes? He said slowly, "I did follow your brothers' tracks."

"You followed their tracks?" He could tell she wanted to be convinced. He remembered her telling him she wanted to believe him.

"But I chose to go hunting in a different direction." That he was hunting for his freedom was a little thing she need not know.

"Where?" she asked suspiciously.

"Your brothers hunted in the gravel hills. I chose to hunt in the pine forest." He found himself hoping she would believe him. He truly did not want to let her know he had run away.

"Then," he continued, "when I discovered the fire in the forest, I came back to warn your people." He waited.

She eyed him suspiciously; then he saw her relax. "*Eeyak*, you did," she agreed readily enough. "You came and helped us." She must have made a decision to believe him, he thought, for the anger seemed to go out of her.

Flint ambled over to them, followed by Dirk and Trout. Blade got to his feet. He doubted her brothers would be as easily convinced.

"He went hunting," Denai said brightly to Flint. "But he went hunting in the pine forest."

"That so?" Flint looked interested. "Get anything?" He eyed Blade challengingly.

"A snakebite," Blade said ruefully.

Flint was silent for a while. Dirk and Trout eyed Blade suspiciously.

"But you came back and warned our people of the fire." Flint's voice was mild. His eyes, however, were hard.

"Eeyak," answered Blade cautiously.

Flint watched him for a time, then, shrugging, he turned away. "Perhaps next time you will think of joining us on the hunt. We know what to do for snakebite." He sauntered off, Dirk and Trout following, and the dog, Sentry, at their heels.

Blade let out a slow breath.

Denai smiled at him. "It is as I told you, Blade. My brothers are very good men," she said. "I think they are pleased that you helped our people."

He grimaced. Great Mother. She thought he wanted to go around pleasing her brothers for the rest of his life.

"I think," he answered, "that your brothers and I see things very differently."

"Perhaps," she acknowledged, "but at least they no longer say you sit around the fire eating the meat others provide." She lifted a brow. "I had wondered if their words bothered you."

"Dak," he lied. "Nothing your brothers say bothers me."

Chapter Sixteen

Denai smiled secretly to herself. She had finished the leggings for Blade!

But should she present them to him? She shuddered as she remembered what had happened to her gift of gray chert stone. He had returned it to Flint.

Even now she squirmed inside whenever she thought of him rejecting her gift. Should she give him the leggings? What if he threw them back at her? Could she withstand that pain again?

Dak, she told herself. She could not. She would not give him the leggings. Not yet.

On the trek, earlier in the day, Blade had killed a sage grouse. Now she was preparing it for the evening meal. The Willow People had traveled slowly this day, but they had made steady progress toward the mammoth water hole.

The place the decision-maker had chosen for them

to camp was near two hills where a small creek bubbled. She could hear the children's happy cries as they splashed the dust off from the day's travel.

Denai hummed as she plucked the bird. Life was good—so much better than before. She had a husband now, and though he did not love her and would one day leave, still, he made her life better. And it was good they were going to a new place where the hunting would be easy. And the day was warm. And she had food.

Sometimes life with the Willow People was not so good. Denai had seen hunger and starvation in her twenty years walking the vast lands. Winters could be cold and snowy. Sometimes the supplies of dried meat ran out. The animals hid in the winter, and it took crafty hunters to bring down a deer or an antelope. Sometimes when there was very little food left among the People, what little they did have was given to the hunters so they could go out and find meat. Sometimes the children died. There had been a severe winter a few years before and three of the little ones and two of the old people had died.

She glanced up at the purpling sky as evening fell. She need not worry about winter now. Now it was warm, it was late summer and there was food. And life was very good.

She finished plucking the bird and buried the entrails. Then she rubbed some herbs on the grouse's skin. She spitted the fowl and leaned it on a stick over the small fire.

That done, she glanced around for Blade and saw him talking to some of the men. She picked up a deer's bladder that she used for carrying water, and walked to the creek.

Theresa Scott

The creek wound its way down among the crevasses between hills and was a small trickle about the span of a man's arm wherever it went. Not large enough to go swimming in, but still it was cool, refreshing water.

Several women and children played in the water, dipping their feet and hands and splashing one another. Little Grasshopper ran up to Denai, her brown eyes dancing. The child threw her arms around Denai.

Denai squeezed her eyes shut, holding Grasshopper close. *Great Mother, let me have a dear child like Grasshopper,* she prayed fervently. *Please!* The short prayer was out before she could stop it.

She smiled down into Grasshopper's eyes. The child hugged her again, then loosened her hold and ran off to play in the water.

Her mother smiled and nodded at Denai. Before Blade had arrived among the Willow People, Grasshopper had been one of the children Denai looked after. But since Blade's arrival, Denai had not cared for a child, not once. Strange how quickly one's life could change, she mused, squatting down to fill the deer bladder.

The water felt cool on her hands. While she waited for the bladder to fill she watched the children play.

She finished filling the bladder and walked slowly among the rocks, over to where Grasshopper's mother sat speaking with another woman. "Grasshopper can take the evening meal with me," Denai offered.

Grasshopper's mother, Moth Wing, nodded her dark head. "She has missed you. I am sure she will enjoy visiting with you."

Denai smiled. "My heart has grown lonely for her, too. She is a good child."

"*Eeyak,* she is," replied the mother.

"You may bring her over to my fireside when you return to camp," Denai suggested.

The woman nodded and Denai left, humming a small tune to herself. She would not let her few friendships lapse while Blade stayed with the Willow People. Once he killed the short-faced bear he would leave and Denai would return to her lonely life. The children she cared for were important in her life and she refused to forget about them. Grasshopper's mother had always seemed kind to Denai, perhaps because she had come to know Denai for herself and not by whatever lies the shaman had told about her.

When Denai reached her hearth, the grouse was dripping fat and the fire was sputtering. She built the flames back up again, then adjusted the stick with the grouse on it.

Blade walked over to join her. "The men are talking about visiting an obsidian site."

"Obsidian?" Denai asked, surprised. "I thought we were going straight to the marsh, the mammoth water hole."

Blade shrugged, sitting down near the fire. "I told them about an obsidian quarry I know of not many days' travel from here. Some of the men want to replenish their rock supplies."

The Willow men were always interested in adding to their rock supplies, Denai knew. Their weapons needed to be made of the best stone they could find, and obsidian, a fine, sharp, volcanic glass, was highly prized to make spear tips and knife blades. The knives cut smoothly and the spear tips penetrated a game animal's hide deeply.

She narrowed her gaze. "You told the men about this obsidian quarry?"

He nodded and stared at the roasting grouse. "When do we eat?"

"Soon," she replied, her mind working. Usually when a man knew about a good quarry for stone, he kept that information to himself or only shared it with trusted friends, often his hunting unit. For Blade to tell the Willow men about an obsidian quarry was a very generous thing for him to do. "That is very kind of you," she observed.

He shrugged and glanced away. He did not want her to think it was important, she realized. Yet it was. His warning about the fire, and now this, his information about the obsidian quarry, all pointed to his gradual acceptance of the Willow People.

And they were growing to accept him, too. Already several people, including Moth Wing, and Rabbit Woman's old mother, had taken Denai aside and whispered their thanks for Blade's timely warning of the fire in the forest. Shyly, both of them had asked her to convey their gratitude to him.

Denai studied him, wondering what it all meant, when Grasshopper came bounding over. "My mother said I may eat with you," she announced.

"*Eeyak*, little one." Denai smiled. "I missed your happy presence and wanted to share meat with you."

Grasshopper plunked herself beside the fire. She sniffed. "Smells good," she said. "I am hungry."

Hiding her smile, Denai took the roasted grouse off the stick and divided the soft meat into three parts. She served Grasshopper, then Blade and then herself. All three ate.

Blade watched Denai with the child. Her eyes softened every time she looked at the girl. And she was thoughtful of the child, too, giving her the meatiest

166

part of the bird and helping break the meat into smaller chunks.

Denai will make a good mother, Blade thought. Then he quashed the thought. Whatever kind of a mother she made was no concern of his. *Dak*, his concern was to kill the short-faced bear. He wondered if taking the Willow People to the obsidian quarry would delay his fight with the bear. It might, if the Willow People moved out of the bear's territory. Bears, however, were known to cover huge territories. He would find the bear.

Blade gnawed on a bone. He had eaten every bite of his share of food. Denai knew how to make meat tasty, that was certain.

He sat back and relaxed, staring at the fire. The trek had gone well this day. The Willow men had listened to him tell of the obsidian quarry. Several of them had been eager to go to visit it, and the decision-maker was one of them.

Wild Dog, the shaman, had glared at Blade, but Blade had no interest in what the shaman did. He had noticed that whenever the shaman appeared, the conversation among the men grew stilted and unnatural. The shaman wielded power among the Willow People. That much was clear. But what kind of power it was, Blade had not determined. It involved fear, however; he knew that much.

The little girl was talking with Denai. If Blade closed his eyes he could pretend that they were a family; he, Denai and the child. This is what it would be like to live with Denai of the Willow People, he thought, opening his eyes. He caught her glance and warm smile. He wondered if she, too, was imagining them as a family.

"I have something for you," Denai said to the child. "Wait."

She walked over to where her baskets were, and rummaged through them. She returned carrying an object longer than her hand.

Blade was curious and sat up a little straighter to see what it was. The girl knew right away what it was and clapped her hands with joy. "A doll!"

Denai smiled and handed the doll to Grasshopper. The child beamed; her round face glowed. "Oh, look!" she cried. "Look at her little dress! It is just like what I wear!"

Denai laughed, a light, happy sound that made Blade happy inside to hear it. He could not take his eyes off her.

The child hugged the doll and Denai hugged her. He wondered if Amethyst had ever given a gift to a child. He did not think that she had.

Denai slid a shy glance at Blade. "I have something for you, too," she said.

"Me?" He shifted uncomfortably.

Her back was to him as she rummaged through her baskets. She turned around and brought something over to him. She squatted down beside him, holding out a folded garment. "Here."

He met her eyes. He saw fear in them, and hope, too. He glanced at the gift. It was made of deer hide, and there were quill decorations and fringe.

"Leggings," she murmured. "For you, for winter."

Knowing that she and the child watched him, he forced himself to take the gift from her hands, though he did not want to. He did not want anything from her. That was why he'd returned the red-striped chert she had tried to give him. He'd felt he had to keep the shirt she had given him during the false marriage ceremony he'd been forced to go through, but he did not want her gifts. And now this.

Another gift. A gift tightened the spiderweb-thin binding between people. A gift meant there was a connection. He did not want a connection with Denai. He had made an agreement that he would kill the bear; that was all. Gifts were not part of the agreement.

"Ooh," murmured the little girl, leaning over to peer at the quillwork Denai had done. "That is pretty. Will you teach me to sew quills like that? My mother says you do the best quillwork of all the Willow women. Even better than Rabbit Woman's, and she's always bragging about her sewing."

Denai blushed at the child's innocent comment.

Blade grunted and drew the leggings closer, showing he intended to keep them. But a sense of hopelessness engulfed him. He should not have returned to the Willow People. He should not be accepting anything from her.

He did not want a wife and he did not need a wife. A feeling of bleakness set in; he did not deserve a wife. If Denai knew what had happened to Amethyst, she would tear these leggings out of his hands and take back the shirt she had sewn as well. And run screaming back to her brothers.

Blade met her eyes and saw the spark of hope residing in her dark, dark eyes. *Do not do this,* he wanted to tell her. *Do not give me presents that will tighten the bonds between you and me.* But he could not say the words. He saw the relief flare in her eyes. *I want nothing from you,* he wanted to say. *I want nothing, and I want to feel nothing! Do you understand?*

He got to his feet and stalked off, away from the

firesides of the Willow People.

He climbed up a small hill. He needed to be alone.

When he got to the top of the hill, he stared down at the leggings he still gripped in both hands. They were folded as she had arranged them and felt soft to his touch.

He wished the bear would find him. Then he could kill it and complete their bargain. And leave!

Chapter Seventeen

Denai had spent a fitful night by the fire. She had not slept well. When Blade had left her fireside last eve, it was only Grasshopper's little hugs that had kept Denai from sobbing like a fool. The child had been happy with her doll, and had not noticed Denai's pain. Denai had accompanied the child back to her mother's fireside, then returned to her own hearth for a long, lonely vigil.

Blade had returned, but he had said nothing to her. He had put away the leggings somewhere. She had been about to ask him why he had left so suddenly when she'd caught a glimpse of his eyes. She saw something so sorrowful and so sad in his dark eyes that the words died in her throat. He had lain down across the fire from her, and when she awoke this morning he had already risen and was working on sharpening his spear points.

"My children," called Uncle Rhino. He raised his arms to catch everyone's attention.

Denai dragged herself over to where the Willow People were gathering.

"I must tell you something," continued the decision-maker. When all had gathered to hear his words, Uncle Rhino said, "My children, we are not going directly to the mammoth water hole. We will make a side trip. I have decided that we must go and see the obsidian quarry that Blade, Denai's new husband, told me about. It is a good place to get rock for making our spearheads and knives."

There were some disappointed murmurs from the women, and satisfied grunts of approval from the men. Denai glanced around. She hoped the quality of the obsidian rock was worth the delay. Like most of the women, she would have preferred to travel onward to the marsh. At the marsh she could swim, fish and snare ducks as well as pick water plants and rushes. But the obsidian quarry was important to the men. And all knew that strong, sharp weapons were important to the well-being of the Willow People, so neither she nor any of the other women protested too strongly.

The Willow People started out, and this time Blade walked in the lead with Uncle Rhino and some of the other men. The rest of the Willow People, women and children and men, were strung out like beads on a necklace behind them.

As she walked, Denai watched Blade talk with the other men. Now and then he gestured to the north. No doubt that was where the obsidian quarry was.

He is a natural leader, she thought. Why had his people let such a valuable and knowledgeable leader go away from them? Had they driven him away or had he been forced to flee them? Had he chosen to leave them? She wished she knew what had happened. Perhaps then she would better understand his behavior to her.

The Willow People stopped in the afternoon for a rest. Denai sat down and was eating some dried meat when Blade walked up to her. She tried to stifle her surprise.

"Are you tired from the walk?" he asked.

She stared at his handsome face; then she said, "*Dak*. Willow women are strong. We can walk for a long time."

He laughed, showing white, white teeth. "I do not doubt it," he agreed.

She tried to ignore the warmth she felt at his words. Sweet words were not going to get her to lower her guard with this man.

"Tell me something," she said. She stopped eating the meat. "Tell me why you left my fireside last night."

He stared into the distance. She thought he was not going to answer, but at last he said, "I did not want to accept your gift."

Tears rose in her eyes and she focused hard on the ground. She did not want him to see her wiping them away. She had worked hard on the pair of leggings, indeed, considered them her best handiwork, and he did not want them!

"Denai," he said, his voice low. "Look at me."

"*Dak*," she said.

"*Eeyak*," he said softly.

The gentleness in his voice made her raise her eyes.

"I think the leggings you made are very fine. They will be very warm when the days grow cold." He hesitated, then plunged on. "I did not want to . . . did not want to accept the gift because I thought it would encourage you to think we are truly husband and wife."

Her face burned hot with her humiliation. "I know you will only stay until the bear is killed," she answered. She wished her voice had not cracked so badly. She shook her hair, striving to make her voice sound uncaring. "I agreed to our bargain. I ask nothing else." *Ah, but I do,* her traitorous heart continued. *I ask that you truly be my husband, that you love me. . . . Stop it!* she commanded her heart. *It can never be! Listen to the pity in his voice. That will tell you all you need to know about the true state of our marriage!*

He was watching her and she thought he knew she lied. He came closer and she could feel the heat of his body, smell the fresh scent of him. She closed her eyes, feeling dizzy.

"Denai," he said softly and lifted her chin. "Please try. . . ." He touched his lips to hers. Her eyes flew open. What . . . ? But then he was kissing her and she closed her eyes, lost in the feeling of his lips, of his touch, of his warmth. She reached up a hand and touched his jaw.

He ended the kiss, and when she opened her eyes he looked as bewildered as she felt. "I did not mean for that to happen—" he began.

"Hush!" She put her fingers over his lips. "Do not say it. Do not say anything." If he were to disavow the kiss, she knew she could not bear it.

She stared into his eyes. He wanted her; she could see it in his hooded gaze. A frisson of desire skipped up her spine. She wanted him, too. Her hand flew to her lips. Oh, how had this happened?

"I must go," he said, stepping away. "I must speak

with the decision-maker." He strode away.

She could not take her eyes off him. All afternoon, as the Willow People trekked to the obsidian quarry, Denai's eyes followed Blade. She wanted him; she wanted him as a husband, as a mate, as a friend. Any way she could get him, she wanted him. She wanted him shamelessly and she knew there was a center deep within her that would do anything, anything to satisfy the longing she had for him. She was not proud of it, she was not pleased with it, but one look at his face and she knew she would do anything to get him or die trying. It was a surprising piece of self-knowledge for her to absorb that afternoon. Never had she felt such a desperate longing for a man.

When she passed Rabbit Woman on the march, she gave the wretched woman a grim smile. They were sisters, of a sort, under the skin. Sisters in desperation. If this was what Rabbit Woman felt every time she looked at Trout, then Denai was surprised the woman had survived so long.

Chapter Eighteen

Why had he kissed her? Whatever had possessed him to kiss her? These questions held Blade's rapt attention as he led the Willow People across the land on the way to the brown obsidian quarry. He had not meant to touch her . . . only to explain. . . . She looked so lovely then, so nervous, so shy, he could not resist. What man could? he asked himself again and again.

He ran his fingers through his hair as he surveyed the horizon. No predators.

He almost wished a lion or a pack of wolves would stalk them. The thrill of the chase would release some of the building frustration he felt. Unfortunately, no predators presented themselves for his satisfaction.

"How much longer to the obsidian quarry?" asked the decision-maker, walking beside Blade.

Blade turned to Uncle Rhino. "We will reach it by nightfall. That is why I suggested it. I knew it would be a short walk for the women and children."

Uncle Rhino nodded, pleased.

Perhaps he should escape again, Blade mused, trekking on. Just run off and leave the Willow People and Denai. That would stop the feelings that had so suddenly, so unexpectedly arisen in him. If he could not see her, he would not want her.

He glanced over his shoulder, testing himself. She walked along, a thoughtful expression on her face. Her black hair blew back from her face, and her cheeks were flushed. Blade realized he might have to travel very far to forget her.

He faced front again, scanning the horizon for landmarks. Ah, yes. The tall rock outcrop in the shape of a tree stump. Soon they would reach the quarry and he could concentrate on showing the men the brown rock that was so excellent for making spears. Then he could forget Denai's face with her lovely dark eyes.

He did not want another wife. He did not need another wife. Amethyst had been enough. Even now, whenever he thought of Amethyst, he felt confusion. She had betrayed him with Hunter. He had loved the woman. His confusion kept getting in the way of his grief. He had thought, until that last day, that she loved him. But the knowledge of what she had done with Hunter hovered over his grief like a buzzard over an antelope carcass. Flapping its wings of jealousy, the buzzard would fly off, only to return and pick at the carcass some more.

He gritted his teeth. What was wrong with him? He had deserted Amethyst, deserted her when she needed him. That was why his people had driven him away. That was what he should be thinking about—his own actions. Not what Amethyst had or had not done.

But whenever he thought about how he'd left her alone, a terrible sadness came over him. She would be alive today if he had not deserted her. A deep shudder shook him. He'd had to leave her that day, had he not?

His jaw clenched and the muscle in his cheek twitched painfully. No matter that he would give his best stone spearhead, the best rock in his possession, to have her alive again. He could not go back and change one thing that had happened. Ever.

He closed his eyes and all he saw was Hunter's enraged face. Hunter holding Amethyst's dead body, her long, black hair dragging the ground. Hunter, his black eyes shards of obsidian as he glared at Blade. How Hunter hated him. Through boyhood they had played, always one with the other. They had grown up together and been the closest of friends.

Until Amethyst. Blade had courted her and so had Hunter. She had chosen Blade. After that, Hunter had become cold and distant with Blade. Though they had still hunted together sometimes, the closeness between them was gone. Something had changed.

Blade sighed. Amethyst. She was what had changed things between Blade and Hunter. Very much. And Blade had been content to let Hunter become distant. It was the price he'd paid for winning Amethyst.

And then her death . . . her death had changed things most of all. After her death had come the time of apartness from his people. A time of loneliness . . .

Blade felt the old anger and sadness, a tight ball of feelings, rise in his chest. *This is what comes of thinking about a woman,* he told himself. *This is what comes of loving a woman.*

* * *

Denai sank wearily to her heels, letting her baskets drop to the ground. At last the Willow People had reached the obsidian quarry.

She glanced around and saw some of the other women beginning to gather brush to make huts for the night. She would rest for just a moment before she started making a hut.

It would be dark soon and she should not wait too long or the hut would have to be made on the morrow.

Uncle Rhino had told her that if the obsidian was of good quality and there was water nearby, the Willow People would stay at the quarry for as many days as she had fingers on one hand. That was fine with Denai.

Her eyes followed Blade as he led Uncle Rhino and her brothers from one rippled clump of obsidian to another. Five days or five and twenty, she did not care. As long as she was near Blade.

She heard Flint's loud exclamation. He was holding up a chunk of dusty brown rock. Several men hurried over. Blade chipped some thin flakes off the obsidian core he held. The men around him began talking excitedly.

Denai saw Trout touch his right hand to Blade's shoulder three times, the customary gesture among Willow men that showed they were friends. Indeed, thought Denai, the rock must be very good. All the men beamed and laughed among themselves.

She smiled to herself, pleased for Blade. It seemed his acceptance among the Willow People was growing day by day. He certainly had *her* acceptance, she thought wryly.

Telling herself she had rested long enough, Denai rose to her feet and began searching the ground for

179

brush she could use to build her hut. She wondered if Blade would share the hut with her; then she quickly quashed the thought.

A glimpse of brown out of the corner of her eye caught her interest. Rabbits. Carefully she unwound the snare she kept with her for such sightings. She swiftly set the snare, then moved away, continuing her hunt for brush in a wide half-circle so that any rabbit, hearing her movements, would run straight into her snare.

After a time it got darker, and Denai found she did not yet have enough brush to make the dwelling. She switched to gathering fuel for a camp fire and soon had a small pile of dried twigs and dried mammoth dung. Evidently a tribe of mammoths had passed this way, leaving behind a rich source of fuel for the Willow Peoples' fires.

When she checked her snare, she found a plump rabbit, caught by the neck.

Denai had a small fire burning when Blade joined her. He glanced at the rabbit she had snared. "I am hungry," he announced, and she smiled at him.

"The rabbit will be cooked soon," she promised softly. How good it was to be able to cook for this man, she thought. Such a little thing, yet so important.

He sat down near her. She observed, "The men sound very pleased with the quarry."

He grunted. "They are. It is good-quality rock. I have been here three times. One time with my people . . ."

He stopped.

She waited, wondering if he would tell her more. It was the first time he'd mentioned his people, other than to deny that he had any.

"Your people?" she prodded, but Blade remained silent. Realizing he would say no more about them, Denai served the rabbit meat. They ate together in silence, and Denai wondered if he would ever speak of the people he had lived with before her brothers had captured him.

She slid a glance at him, and saw him staring warily at something behind her. She swiveled around. "Oh no," she murmured.

The shaman came toward them. Wild Dog walked slowly, and leaned on his stick every step of the way. Bchind him trailed Rabbit Woman and Pika and some of the Willow People.

The shaman and fire-keeper halted when he came abreast of Denai's fireside. "Ho!" he greeted.

"What is it?" Denai asked. Blade nodded a silent greeting. The shaman ignored her and glared at Blade.

"So." Wild Dog sneered. "You think you are such a strong man? A smart man?" Anger churned through the shaman's words.

Blade said nothing, only watched the shaman. Denai stirred uneasily. She glanced around for Trout or Flint, but her brothers were clustered around a piece of rock some distance away.

"People in this camp talk about you," continued the shaman in a venomous voice. "They say you led us to a good rock quarry." The shaman spat in disgust. "I say the rock is useless." He threw down a piece of obsidian that split in half in a way that made the stone utterly useless.

Blade got to his feet and picked up one of the broken shards. "This stone has been deliberately cracked," he said evenly, meeting the shaman's angry gaze.

"*Dak!* It was poor-quality rock to begin with. Anyone knows that."

"You may be able to crack this piece," Blade said, hefting the obsidian in his hand. "But it will take you a long time to crack your way through the whole quarry."

Some of the people behind the shaman snickered.

Red faced, the shaman said angrily, "Some of these Willow People think you are such a fine man. They say that you warned us about the fire."

Denai swallowed nervously. What was the shaman up to?

Wild Dog leaned forward, his eyes like glowing coals in his face. "You set the fire! That is how you knew to warn us. Because you set it!"

"Dak," Blade answered calmly. "The lightning from the sky set the forest on fire. The forest was very dry, the wood dry. . . ."

"You set it!" the shaman screamed. "The magpie came and told me that you set it. You lied to my people! You are not the good man everyone thinks you are!"

Denai heard some grumblings behind Wild Dog. She saw some of the men and women of the Willow People regarding Blade suspiciously.

Blade sat down. "Think what you want," he answered carelessly.

"No!" Denai cried, jumping to her feet. "Blade would not set the fire! He is an honorable man. He came to warn us! He saved our lives, even your life." She swung on the shaman, pointing at him. "Is this how you speak to the man who saved your life?"

"He did not save my life," cried the shaman. "I would have wakened in time. I did not need his help."

"The magpie would have wakened him," joked Rabbit Woman. Pika giggled.

The shaman growled at her and the two women glanced nervously away.

"I say that you set the fire, stranger. I say that you led us to a pitiful rock place. I would not even call it a quarry!"

There was an unmistakable challenge in the shaman's voice. Denai recognized it; she wondered if Blade did.

"Any man who uses this rock," the shaman continued, "will fail to bring down a deer. The antelope will easily escape his spear if the tip is made of this rock. And mammmoths! Ha! Mammoths will turn and trample any man who uses this obsidian! That is what your power is, stranger. Puny. Weak. Not like mine. Mine is strong. Mine knows what is the truth!"

The Willow People were silent, watching Blade and the shaman.

Denai shifted from foot to foot uneasily. Somehow, she was not sure how, Blade had made an enemy of the shaman. Just as she had. Now the venom of his hatred poured upon Blade. She had experienced the shaman's hatred, and knew the hardships he could visit upon someone he hated. She did not want that for Blade.

She stepped forward. "You are mistaken, esteemed fire-keeper," she said respectfully. "This man, my new husband, did not intend to hurt any of us. He sought only to warn us. To help us. He is an honorable man." She turned pleading eyes on the shaman.

He glared at her. "Do not think to cajole me, woman! I know the truth!" He glared at Blade. "I know this man is not what he seems! Someday you will learn just how much he has lied to us!"

Denai shook her head at Wild Dog uneasily. What did he know about Blade?

Blade stared at Denai. She was trying to defend him, he thought in amusement. She was trying to placate this evil old man. Well, he did not need her defense. He did not need anyone's. His leg twitched and he remembered the snakebite. Perhaps he did need people.

His amusement faded. She had told the old fire-keeper that he, Blade, was an honorable man. What did she know? Guilt pricked at him. An honorable man would never have left his wife to die.

The shaman was right. There were things about him that the Willow People did not know. And would not accept if they did know.

He waved a hand at Denai, at the shaman. "Let him be," he said to Denai, hoping the old man would go away.

The shaman smiled, a slow, evil smile. "He is afraid of me," he said approvingly. Wild Dog turned and cackled to the Willow People, who listened. "*Eeyak*, he is afraid of me!"

Chapter Nineteen

The Willow People had been at the quarry for two days. The shaman's accusations of faulty obsidian had had little effect. The men were happy; several sang as they chipped away at chunks of the shiny brown rock, forming them into the tools they would need—tools such as knives, spear points and scrapers for scraping hides. The men also made blanks, which were more roughly shaped pieces that could be finely worked later into a knife or spear point. Sometimes the men made two-faces. Two-faces were large pieces of rock that flakes could be chipped off of. Two-faces could also be broken into two pieces and each of those worked into a tool. Several little boys skipped around the men, reaching for the cast-off flakes.

Denai watched Blade. He sat with a group of men that included her brothers. They all intently flaked cores of brown obsidian. Occasionally a man would say something, but for the most part they were silent as they concentrated on their delicate work.

Sitting by her brush hut and sewing a pair of moccasins for the oncoming winter, Denai was content to stare at Blade as often as she wanted. He, of course, did not know she watched him. He also did not know of her disappointment that he slept outside her hut at night.

Sometimes he chipped countless flakes off a rock just to get one perfect spear tip. Denai marveled at his patience.

On the first day of the Willow People's stay at the quarry, Uncle Rhino had asked the shaman to sing a song of thanks to the Great Mother for guiding the Willow People to such a find. Unfortunately the shaman refused and stalked off in anger. Some of the Willow People were upset that he had not said the prayer of thanks; others thanked the Great Mother themselves.

Denai thought it mattered little what the shaman did. She did not, however, say her own prayer of thanks, because she believed the Great Mother was angry with her. Why else would Chert, her betrothed, have been killed? Yet even Denai could understand the gratitude in her uncle's heart when he had asked Wild Dog to say the prayer. The obsidian quarry truly was a gift to her people, and she knew they would carry away as much of the rock as they could.

Two of the hunting units, including her brothers', planned to leave at dawn on the third day to go hunting. The Willow People needed meat so they could stay at the quarry for the full five days Uncle Rhino had planned.

Denai watched from her sleeping mat as Blade conferred with her brothers. They used hand gestures to keep from waking those around them. She could barely see his dim silhouette in the early dawn light. The men were anxious to try out their new spear points on game.

Bringing the Willow People to the quarry had strengthened Blade's ties with her brothers. She could see that. No longer did Flint tell Sentry to guard Denai from Blade.

And it would not have done any good if he had, thought Denai, for she had seen Blade feeding meat to the dog whenever he thought no one was looking. No longer did the huge beast growl when he saw Blade; now he wagged his tail like a puppy. Denai smiled to herself as she watched Blade pick up his spears and saunter silently off with her brothers for the hunt.

She lay back down and closed her eyes. Blade had won the dog's trust. He had won her brothers' approval. She ran a finger gently over her lips. And what about Denai? The tears welling up in her eyes gave answer enough.

It was a good thing they were going hunting, Blade thought. He could not have taken much more of lying outside Denai's brush hut and listening to her rhythmic breathing. How could the woman sleep when all he could think about was how close she was—but an arm's length away—about how soft her skin was, how beautiful her eyes, how full her breasts, of how he would like to mate with—Stop it! he ordered himself.

He felt sweat spring to his brow despite the cool morning air. He glanced over his shoulder, back at her brush hut. Why did he have to go hunting? some way-

187

ward part of him wanted to know. Why could he not stay with Denai?

Flint saw the gesture and said firmly, "The sooner we find meat, the sooner we may return."

"Blade wants to stay at camp and let us do his hunting for him," said Trout with feigned innocence.

Blade glared at him, but the younger Willow man, undaunted, broke into a laugh. Dirk laughed, too. Finally Blade cracked a smile.

The mood among the four men was amiable as they walked along, looking for antelope or deer tracks. Blade bent to the ground and touched a track. Mammoths had been this way, he saw, and his senses perked up. He counted the tracks of seven adults and two calves. He saw, too, by the freshness of their dung, that it was within the last seven days that they had passed this way. That surprised him. Everyone knew mammoths preferred to stay near water holes. There was not much water in this area; indeed, the only water he knew of was the creek back at the obsidian quarry where the Willow People were camped.

Perhaps this mammoth herd had become lost, though that did not happen often. Usually they went from water hole to water hole; the big matriarchs that led the herds remembered paths from seasons past.

Blade preferred to hunt mammoths at water holes. They were easier to hunt when their huge round feet were caught in the soft mud and they were sinking. Then a hunter had a very good chance of bringing one down, even if he was alone.

"What is that?" Dirk pointed to the sky.

"Vultures," Trout answered tersely.

The men hurried forward, wondering what prey the vultures had found.

They walked up a small rise in the land and halted. The huge birds circled a mammoth carcass.

Curious, the men loped forward. When they reached the carcass, the stench caused Trout to grab his nose dramatically and fall to the ground as if overcome by the smell.

The bones of the animal lay exposed and it was obvious that lions and wolves had dragged the vertebrae apart to get at the meat. The bones had been stripped, too, probably by the wolves and lions that had discovered it. Now there were only small rodents nibbling at the shreds of meat still left on the bones. Mice ran off with angry squeaks when the men approached.

"Ho! We disturbed their breakfast," Trout said, scrambling to his feet. "They do not like that." He threw a stone at an escaping rat.

"You missed," Dirk noted dryly. "Your aim needs work."

The Willow men poked around the carcass. Blade was curious, too. He prodded a bone aside, wondering if the animal had been brought down by men or if it had been diseased or injured and predators had killed it.

"Nothing much here," Flint decided at last. "Let us go and find a deer. Our people will be hungry this day."

He turned away from the carcass, as did Trout and Dirk. Blade gave one last prod with his spear when he noticed a dark gleam on the ground.

The others were walking away. "Come, Blade," called Trout. "We can find you something better to eat than that!"

Flint guffawed.

Ignoring them, Blade knelt down. He picked up a spear point. Obsidian.

189

"What is it?" Flint asked, eyeing him.

Blade enclosed the spear point carefully in his hand and got to his feet. "Just a toe bone," he answered carelessly. "Want it?"

"No thanks," Trout quipped, "I have ten of my own."

Flint snorted. "Come, Trout," he said. "The deer call us."

The three brothers quickened their pace away from the carcass.

Blade followed after them, thoughtful. In his hand he held a cold, sharp spear point. He recognized the workmanship. It was made by Hunter of the Lion People.

Chapter Twenty

Sentry barked. Denai looked up and saw her brothers enter the Willow camp. Each one proudly carried a skinned and gutted deer. Blade trailed behind them, an eviscerated antelope over one broad shoulder. His long, muscular legs covered the ground rapidly. He brushed his dark hair off his face with one hand and steadied the carcass with the other. The muscles in his arms bulged with strength.

Denai's heart pounded.

He lowered the animal to the ground and began quartering it. Each of her brothers quartered the deer they had brought in. Happy cries went up from the gathered Willow People. They would eat well this day and the next.

Denai watched Blade. He knelt on the ground and made smooth, swift movements as he cut through the antelope meat and bone. He glanced in her direction and hesitated. Then he went back to butchering the antelope. He cut out the animal's tongue and gestured to Denai. She hurried forward, knowing he meant for her to take it. The tongue was one of the tastiest delicacies of the antelope.

Her hand trembled as she took the proffered meat. "You—you have had much success," she murmured to him. His hand touched hers as he gave her the meat. Her eyes widened. "I—I will cook this up. I will roast it in hot embers in the fire. I will clean it well beforehand. I—I must go down to the creek," she babbled, not knowing or caring if her words made sense.

He stopped cutting the meat and regarded her speculatively, those dark eyes of his revealing nothing. He smiled slowly and her heart turned over. Her breath . . . Why could she no longer breathe?

Then he returned to butchering the antelope. She could breathe again. Inhaling, she realized she was close enough to smell his salty, smoky scent. She closed her eyes and breathed in deeply. Ah, but he smelled good.

She opened her eyes to find him staring at her. His mouth tilted in a small half-smile on one side of his face. She stared. She'd seen him smile so seldom.

"Do you want something else?" he asked.

"*Dak!*" she cried in mortification, and fled toward her brush hut. When she got there she had to brace herself against a scraggly pine tree for a moment to catch her breath. Whatever was wrong with her?

Finally, her heartbeat restored to its normal pace, she set about gathering fuel for a fire. She scanned the ground for twigs and dug up some roots. She would not look at him; she would not.

She went over to the fire-keeper. He sullenly followed her back to her fireside. He carried with him a twisted sage knot. The knot housed several smoldering embers. The shaman took a stick and scraped an ember out of the tiny shelter. The ember landed in the shavings Denai had prepared. The shaman left and she felt relieved.

She coaxed the ember to become a fire. That done, she checked the water bladders. They were empty, so she took them and the antelope tongue down to the stream. She filled the bladders and scrubbed the tongue thoroughly, then carried them all back to her hearth.

The fire crackled, and there were enough hot coals to roast the meat. She sat down and rewarded herself with a swift glance at Blade.

He was talking with her brothers. They were laughing at something one of them had said.

She had to gather some things to make the evening meal. Why then, she scolded herself, was she still sitting here, content to stare only at Blade? The usual things—the meat, the roots, the herbs, even making an offer of meat to her neighbors—none of it concerned her. Only Blade did.

She raised the back of her hand to her mouth.

Something was very wrong with her. She wondered who she could ask about it. If she continued in this manner she would wither up and die at her fireside, her eyes focused on that man even in her death.

Stop it! she commanded herself sternly. *Take your eyes off him; get up and go and find the herbs you need to flavor the antelope meat!* Unwillingly, she struggled to her feet. Despite her intentions, her traitorous eyes sought him out. Ah, but he was good to look at. . . .

Perhaps if she just glanced at him now and then.

That is it, she thought, watching him out of the corner of her eye. *If I only watch him now and then, I can still work and—*

"Sister?"

She jumped guiltily. "What is it?" She rounded on Trout. "What are you doing sneaking up on me like a lion does a deer?"

He looked bewildered at her charge. "I do not mean to sneak," he said. "I merely wanted to tell you something."

She frowned at him, irritated. "What do you wish to say?"

"It is about your new husband."

She took a step closer to Trout, worried now. "What about him? Is he not a good hunter? Are you sorry you gave him to me?" she asked in alarm.

He laughed and waved her back down. "Hush, Sister. It is not that. He is a fine hunter. He is patient, he knows the tracks, he is fine," Trout soothed. "But his leg, he ignores it and I think it is swelling. I thought perhaps you could put some leaves on it to heal it."

"Oh! *Eeyak.* I-I meant to," she said. "But he told me it did not hurt."

"He said that?" Trout looked surprised. "I noticed him limping."

"I will get the leaves," she said, practically pushing Trout away from her hearth in her haste. "Go! I will get them right now!"

She hurried away from her hut. She had seen some healing leaves growing down near the creek. She had but to pick a few.

When she returned with the healing leaves, she found Blade sitting at her fireside. "Greetings," she said, clutching the leaves to her chest. "I-I was just gathering some leaves—"

"I am hungry," he announced, glancing pointedly at the fire. "Where is the meat?"

She frowned. Clearly there was no meat cooking. She stirred the embers, then carefully placed the roots and antelope tongue in the hot coals. Satisfied that the meal would cook, she said, "I must look at your leg. I want to make sure it is healing from the snakebite."

He winced. "It is fine."

"Let me look."

"*Dak.*"

"*Eeyak.*" She met his eyes defiantly. Brown eyes glared into black eyes.

She was surprised when he admitted, "It does hurt, but only a little."

His lower leg was red and puffy. If her leg were like this, she would be crying out in pain, thought Denai.

She pounded the healing leaves into a green mass and spread it over his calf near where the snake's fangs had first pierced his flesh.

"There, we must leave that on your leg throughout the night. These mashed leaves will draw out the poison. You should feel much less pain by morning."

She thought he looked grateful, but only for a heartbeat.

They sat looking at the tiny flames, waiting for the meat to cook. Now and then her eyes slid of their own will in his direction. He was staring hard at the fire.

"Where did you learn to heal?" he asked, breaking the silence at last. She thought he turned his eyes to her reluctantly.

"From my grandmother," she answered. "She is dead now. But after my mother died, my grandmother taught me how to sew, how to cook, and which were the best plants for healing."

"You learned well," Blade observed.

Denai blushed and her eyes sought the ground. "Thank you," she murmured.

He touched his leg at the knee, just above the puffy area. "My first wife, Amethyst, did not know anything about healing."

Denai glanced up in surprise. "Y-your first wife?" she stammered. She remembered that he had mentioned her before. Once. The time when he had taunted her brothers about Denai's lack of beauty.

Denai leaned forward. "Amethyst . . . It is a beautiful name. Do you miss her very much?" she asked, holding her breath, and hoping the answer would be *dak*.

"I think about her every day." Why did he sound so bitter?

Denai stared at the ground. She had not wanted to hear those words. She picked up a stick and poked listlessly at the embers.

"My wife died while we were camping near a river," Blade said softly. "Just the two of us. I left camp for a time. When I returned she was gone. We were upriver from our people. I returned to my people and found her drowned."

Denai met his eyes. "You told me once that you loved her and hated her."

"It is true. I do," he admitted slowly.

"Could—could you ever find it in your heart to love another woman?" Denai blurted. She clasped her hands tightly. Oh, what was the matter with her? Why had she asked such a thing? She should clap her hands over her mouth and never speak again if such foolish words were going to burst forth from her!

Only silence met her outburst. When she looked up at Blade he was staring at the fire. "When will that meat be ready?" he asked.

"Soon," she answered, sadness settling around her heart.

In the silence that followed there was only the crackling sound of fire eating wood.

"It was because of my wife's death that my people drove me away," Blade said at last.

Denai glanced up, tentative hope creeping through her breast, hope that he would continue to talk to her, to tell her of himself, his life, his people. . . .

"Your people are fools," she cried. Her voice trembled with anger. She started to rise to her feet, but caught herself. "They drove away a strong leader when they pushed you away! They are fools!"

Blade snorted. "They were happy. They said they were getting rid of a man who would not help his wife. A man who left his wife to die. Left her alone."

"They said that?" whispered Denai, aghast.

"*Eeyak.*"

"Were they right?" She held her breath.

He gazed at her, his black eyes veiling his thoughts. Then he swung his head and stared at the fire. After some time she realized he was not going to answer her. She rose and took the meat and roots from the embers.

They ate their meal in silence, but Denai's thoughts raced. He had told her some things about himself. Given time, perhaps he would tell her more. Did he not know she wanted only to love him?

* * *

Blade set aside the last bit of tongue meat, too upset to eat any more. Great Mother, what had possessed him to tell Denai about Amethyst and her death and his people?

He glanced over at her, sitting on the other side of the fire. She met his eyes slowly. He wondered what was behind those beautiful dark eyes. Was there contempt or . . . or was there, perhaps, understanding?

Strange, how he wanted to tell her about himself. She was so quiet. He had been accustomed to a woman who chattered like a magpie. But Denai did not chatter. She was silent unless she had something important to say. Or—he grinned to himself—unless she was flustered by him, like today, when he had handed her the antelope tongue. Then she babbled.

He shifted his sore leg a little. He hoped the mashed leaves would cure his leg. A hunter needed both legs. Though he had tried to keep from limping around her brothers as much as possible, at times the leg hurt so much he limped anyway. He supposed one of them had told her.

He was glad she was trying to help heal his leg. It made him feel kindly toward her. And she had looked so concerned when he'd told her how his people drove him away. She had wanted to defend him. She had actually looked ready to jump up from her fireside to go and scold the Lion People.

Ah, the Lion People. Now that he had seen Hunter's abandoned spear point, he knew they were in the area. Had they already seen the Willow People? It was possible they did not know the Willow People were here.

He remembered the first time his people had seen a group of new people wandering in the distance. Blade had been but a boy at the time, and his father was the accepted headman of the Lions. Liontooth, his father, had advised that they approach the new people carefully. He had warned that they might want to trade skins or weapons with the Lion People or that they might want to fight. Few had heeded Liontooth. Some of the Lion People, including Ochre, excited at seeing the new people, had rushed up to them.

Frightened, the new people had raised their weapons. Some of their young boys had thrown stones, and one of the Lion People, an elderly woman, had been hurt. After that, Ochre had screamed ferociously at the strangers. One of their men, a heavy, bearded stranger, had thrown a spear at Ochre, and then he and the rest of them had run away.

It was a long time before the Lion People saw any more strangers. By then Blade was a young man. This time the Lion People were very cautious. Liontooth went forth to speak with them by himself. The talk had gone well and the two groups of people had been able to trade.

How, mused Blade, would the Lions approach the Willow People?

Knowing the Lion People, they would be cautious— if Liontooth was still alive. But if Ochre or Hunter, or one of the other impetuous men, was leading them they might try to sneak up on the Willow People. Blade would have to be alert for any more signs of them.

Sadly, he wondered if his father was still alive. It had been over two summers since he'd been forced to leave the Lion People, and his father had looked old and frail even then. By now Liontooth must already have passed on to the fireside of the Great Mother.

Blade glanced over at Denai. So much to think

about, he mused. The fire had died down, and there were few sounds coming from the other brush huts. The Willow People had retired for the night.

Denai watched him out of huge brown eyes. He could not bear for her to creep into her brush hut this night and leave him alone outside again.

He held out a hand to her, palm open, fingers splayed. She touched his hand and he nodded, encouraging her. He closed his fingers around hers. "Please," he entreated. "Sleep beside me this night. I will keep you warm."

Her eyes searched his. Slowly she nodded and came over to him. She knelt down beside him. Blade dared not even breathe. "Thank you," he whispered softly. "I did not want to be alone tonight." Her eyes were solemn and then she nodded.

He lay down, bringing her with him so that her back was to him. He put an arm across her stomach and closed his eyes, holding her. She smelled of woodsmoke and sagebrush and womanly warmth. It had been too long since he'd held a woman, he realized. Too, too long.

Though he wanted to pull her close to him, he resisted. She might become afraid, and he would do nothing to frighten her away this night. Instead he willed himself to be satisfied with holding her. After a while he felt her relax, heard her soft breathing. Then he, too, was able to fall asleep.

Chapter Twenty-one

"No!" Denai cried. "*Dak!*" She thrashed back and forth, trying to dislodge the bear's grip on her arm. "Do not take me with you!" she cried. Her body shook with fear.

"Denai! Wake up," came an urgent voice. "Wake up!"

She flung out her arms. The bear! It was after her! She must get away!

"Denai!"

Panting in fear, she struggled against the arm that held her. Then she opened her eyes. It was Blade she was fighting. "How . . . ? Who . . . ?" she tried.

He stroked her hair. "You had a frightening dream."

She shook her head, trying to dispel the image of the bear. It had been so real. The short-faced bear had been right there. He chased her, his wide-open mouth exposing sharp yellow teeth, his roars loud in her ears.

She ran and ran, but he caught her.

Trembling, she sat up.

Blade's warm hand stroked her shoulder. "It was a frightening dream," he repeated.

She shrugged off his touch and he drew his hand back. Her shoulder felt cold. "It was nothing," she murmured, looking down at the ground.

If it was nothing, why am I shaking so? she asked herself. *The bear seemed so real, but it was a dream. Why then, do I still tremble?*

She rose to her feet, swaying, and put a hand to her head. "I must—I must get away," she whispered.

She looked around wildly. Where could she hide? The brush hut? The bear would find her. The creek? *Dak,* he could easily drag her away from there. Where then?

Her gaze fell upon Blade and a calmness seemed to come over her. Perhaps she would be safe with him. He watched her, a puzzled look on his face. She closed her eyes. She could not tell him; she could not! He would think her a frightened fool, afraid of her own dreams.

"I must hide," she muttered and staggered off, she knew not where.

He followed her. "Denai?" When she stumbled he reached for her. "Denai. It was a dream. You are awake now."

She shook her head, trying to shake off the strong hold the dream had upon her. "I saw it; it chased me."

"What chased you?"

She saw him then. Blade. Truly saw him. His dark eyes held concern. Still frightened by her dream, she tried to pull away from him, out of his arms. "I cannot say."

He frowned. "Very well, do not tell me. But whatever it was, you are safe here."

"Am I?" she asked, but the question was meant for herself. Was she safe here with the Willow People? Or would the bear, Evil One, find her and kill her and— Oh, no!

She stared at Blade, the sleepiness fleeing from her in the wake of a new fear. Oh, no! The bear! She had forgotten. It would chase Blade and kill him, too! The shaman had said the bear would kill any man who chose her as a mate. She had refused to believe it before.

But this dream had convinced her otherwise. The bear was real. He had killed Chert. And he was coming for Denai. And Blade.

She bit her lip. Oh, what should she do? She had dragged Blade into her troubles. By marrying her he had put himself in danger. He was not safe as long as he was here, with her, and with her people.

Calm yourself, she told herself sharply. *You have made a bargain with him. He will kill the bear.*

No, muttered some deep, frightened part of her. *No one can kill this bear. It is too strong! Any bear that can enter a woman's dreams and chase her very soul has a power stronger than a mere man's, even if the man is Blade.*

She whirled from him then and ran into her brush hut. Feeling her way through her baskets, she pulled out what she sought. Her knife.

A knife is no protection from a bear, she scoffed inwardly. "But I must do something," she protested aloud. "I cannot let Evil One kill me!" And it was Evil One in her dream. She had recognized the hairless patch of skin on his right flank.

She clutched the knife tightly in her fist. She would keep the knife with her, she vowed. Day and night she would have that knife. She would use it to defend herself!

As the day wore on, the memory of the dream stayed with her. Throughout the time she gathered twigs for the fire, throughout the time she fetched water and made the midday meal, throughout the time she gathered roots, still the dream haunted her.

By late afternoon she was exhausted and fearful. The root she was trying to pull out of the ground would not come out even with the aid of her digging stick. It did not help her efforts that every now and then she had to stop and survey the land around her, prepared to run the moment she saw the bear.

She set her digging stick aside and tugged futilely on the stubborn root. Suddenly a deep voice beside her made her jump. "Denai?"

"Blade!"

He eyed her questioningly.

"I . . . I did not hear your footsteps." She faltered.

He smiled slowly. "Is there anything left of that root?"

She glanced down at her handiwork. The root was shredded from her efforts with her digging stick, and the top green leaves had all been yanked and squeezed off where she had been trying to drag it out of the ground. "*Dak*," she muttered in disgust, letting go of the plant. "There is nothing on it worth eating now."

He chuckled and helped her to her feet. "Come. You have set aside enough roots for the next meal. Let us walk together."

She glanced around fearfully. "I want to stay close to the Willow People."

He said nothing, but watched her pick up her digging stick and tools. "A knife, Denai?" He frowned. "I do not recall you carrying such a sharp knife with you."

"I . . . I do not." She flushed. "But I do now."

"Did something happen that frightened you?"

She wanted to close her eyes against the gentleness she heard in his voice. Finally, with a slump of her shoulders, she gave up the struggle. What did it matter if he knew the worst about her? Knew that she was a fear-filled coward? *"Eeyak,"* she murmured. "I am afraid. I am very afraid."

He straightened and she noticed the spear he carried. The point was sharp brown obsidian, and the long wooden handle was colored in red and black stripes to make the spear fly faster. A spear like that could protect a woman.

When he did not laugh at her, or scoff, as she had expected, she added in a tiny voice, "It was my dream. I was chased." She could not say any more. She closed her eyes, remembering the bear's growls, his breath on her heels as he chased her, the powerful grip of his arms. . . .

"Who chased you?" Blade asked patiently.

Her eyes flew open. "The bear. Evil One." She shuddered.

"The bear the shaman spoke of?"

She nodded. "The bear that killed Chert. The bear that the shaman says will return to kill me."

He frowned. "How does the shaman know this?"

She shrugged. "He knows. Birds tell him things. Animals tell him things. I do not know all the ways he knows about things. But he is a cruel man. I do not go and talk with him about these things. I do not want

205

to know how he gets his knowledge."

"That is wise," Blade agreed. "From what I have seen of the man, I think he would tell you something false to try to scare you. I think he likes telling people that bad things will happen to them."

Denai nodded. "He frequently tells us bad news."

"Perhaps he thinks it is the only way he can be a leader among your people."

Denai glanced at Blade. "Perhaps."

"It does make people listen." He observed her closely. "You listen to him."

She frowned. "I listen to the bear," she objected. "The bear was the one in my dream. Not the shaman. The bear was the one who chased me."

"I was chased by a bear once. I did not like it."

She glanced at him. "I did not like it in my dream, either."

"No. Bears are powerful," he agreed.

Denai slid a glance at Blade. She liked the way he listened to her. He is a kind man, she thought. She did not feel so foolish now.

"Let us walk over by the creek for a while," she suggested.

He nodded. Denai put the roots in her small basket, picked up her digging stick and tied her knife at her waist. They sauntered along. Denai patted her knife. She did not feel so fearful of the bear now. Her knife and Blade would keep the bear away. She hoped.

Children played in the cool water and mothers chatted with one another as Denai and Blade strolled past them.

They followed the stream for a short distance, and Denai found a place where the creek widened. She sat on a rock and dangled her feet in the cool liquid. She closed her eyes. "Ah, the water feels good," she said.

Blade nodded and smiled. "Water is precious," he agreed. He glanced at the plants and small trees growing beside the creek. "Everything depends upon it. Plants, animals, birds, you, me."

He leaned back against a rock and closed his eyes. "Come and sit beside me," he said, patting the ground beside him. His eyes were still closed.

Denai paddled her feet in the water.

"Perhaps," he said lazily, opening his eyes, "I will have to come and get you."

She jumped to her feet and ran. He raced after her. She could hear him behind her.

"I will catch you!" he cried.

She ran faster. But in another moment he swooped her up into his arms in midstride. She gave a squeal of delight. His strong arms caught her close to him. Giggling, she looked up into his eyes.

"Caught you!" he crowed.

She laughed happily. "I will get away!"

She tickled him under the arms and broke from his embrace. He let her go easily and then ran after her, only to snatch her up again. Laughing, he threw her over his shoulder. She stared at the ground and kicked weakly as he marched back to the creek. He placed her carefully on her feet. "Now!" he said, panting. "You will sit beside me!"

With a giggle she plopped down onto the ground. He dropped down beside her and put his arms around her. He leaned into her, kissing her. Ah, but his kiss was sweet.

She smiled to herself and kissed him again.

They spent the rest of the afternoon kissing and dangling their feet in the water.

Holding hands, they walked back to camp. Denai made a fire. While the roots were cooking, Trout hurried up to them. "Denai!"

"What is it?" Denai asked, glancing up from poking at the roasting roots.

"One of our hunters, Turtle, has been hurt! He needs help!"

"Hurt?" Denai cried. "What happened?"

Trout hesitated. "He has many cuts," he said finally.

She glanced at Blade. "I must go to the creek. The healing leaves grow there."

"I will go with you," Blade offered.

They hurried to the creek and picked the leaves. On the way back Denai confided to Blade, "I fear Turtle is badly hurt. My brother did not want to tell me how badly."

They reached the brush hut where Turtle, his wife and two children lived. Turtle, a man of middle age, lay on his back, unconscious. His wife, looking worried, sat next to him and sang quietly under her breath. Denai heard the words. The woman was praying.

"What happened?" Denai asked, kneeling down beside the injured man. His forearm had several deep gouges. With dread, Denai realized they were scratches from a huge paw. She must work quickly if she was going to keep the hot sickness from entering his arm. Hunters needed both arms.

"What happened?" she asked again, glancing up at Trout.

He shrugged. "He was attacked by a bear."

Dread was pounding its terrifying song in Denai's